The International Spv

Allen Upward

Contents

Prologue—the Two Empresses.................................... 5

Chapter 1 The Instructions of Monsieur V——.................. 11

Chapter 2 The Princess Y——'s Hint........................... 17

Chapter 3 The Head of the Manchurian Syndicate.............. 27

Chapter 4 The Czar's Autograph............................... 34

Chapter 5 A Dinner With the Enemy........................... 41

Chapter 6 Drugged and Kidnapped............................. 48

Chapter 7 The Race for Siberia............................... 54

Chapter 8 The Czar's Message................................. 58

Chapter 9 The Betrothal of Delilah........................... 67

Chapter 10 The Answer of the Mikado......................... 75

Chapter 11 Who Smoked the Gregorides Brand................. 84

Chapter 12 The Secret Service of Japan....................... 89

Chapter 13 His Imperial Highness............................. 97

Chapter 14 The Submarine Mine............................... 103

Chapter 15 The Advisor of Nicholas II........................ 110

Chapter 16 A Strange Confession............................. 115

Chapter 17 A Supernatural Incident.......................... 126

Chapter 18 The Mystery of a Woman........................... 134

Chapter 19 The Spirit of Madame Blavatsky................... 143

Chapter 20 The Devil's Auction.............................. 153

Chapter 21 The Funeral...................................... 159

Chapter 22 A Perilous Moment................................ 168

Chapter 23 A Resurrection and a Ghost....................... 174

Chapter 24 A Secret Execution............................... 179

Chapter 25 A Change of Identity............................. 186

Chapter 26 Trapped.. 191

Chapter 27 The Baltic Fleet................................. 196

Chapter 28 On the Track.. 204

Chapter 29 An Imperial Fanatic............................. 211

Chapter 30 The Stolen Submarine......................... 218

Chapter 31 The Kiel Canal..................................... 224

Chapter 32 The Dogger Bank................................. 231

Chapter 33 Trafalgar Day....................................... 236

Chapter 34 The Family Statute............................... 241

Epilogue.. 248

Prologue—the Two Empresses

"Look!"

A fair, delicately-molded hand, on which glittered gems worth a raja's loyalty, was extended in the direction of the sea.

Half a mile out, where the light ripples melted away into a blue and white haze upon the water, a small black smudge, like the back of a porpoise, seemed to be sliding along the surface.

But it was not a porpoise, for out of it there rose a thin, black shaft, scarcely higher than a flag-staff, and from the top of this thin shaft there trickled a faint wreathing line of smoke, just visible against the background of sky and sea.

"It is a submarine! What is it doing there?"

The exclamation, followed by the question, came from the second, perhaps the fairer, of two women of gracious and beautiful presence, who were pacing, arm linked in arm, along a marble terrace overlooking a famous northern strait.

The terrace on which they stood formed part of a stately palace, built by a king of the North who loved to retire in the summer time from his bustling capital, and gather his family around him in this romantic home.

From here, as from a watch-tower, could be seen the fleets of empires, the crowded shipping of many a rich port and the humbler craft of the fisherman, passing and repassing all day long between the great inland sea of the North and the broad western ocean.

Along this narrow channel had once swept the long ships of the Vikings, setting forth on those terrible raids which devastated half Europe and planted colonies in England and

France and far-off Italy. But to-day the scene was a scene of peace. The martial glory of the Dane had departed. The royal castle that stood there as if to guard the strait had become a rendezvous of emperors and queens and princes, who took advantage of its quiet precincts to lay aside the pomp of rule, and perhaps to bind closer those alliances of sovereigns which serve to temper the fierce rivalries of their peoples.

The pair who stood gazing, one with curiosity and wonder, the other with an interest of a more painful character, at the sinister object on the horizon, were imperial sisters. Born in the tiny sea kingdom, they had lived to wear the crowns of the greatest two realms the world has ever seen, two empires which between them covered half the surface of our planet, and included one-third of its inhabitants.

But though sundered in interests they were not divided in affection. As they stood side by side, still linked together, it was evident that no common sympathy united them.

The one who had been first to draw attention to the mysterious craft, and whose dress showed somber touches which spoke of widowhood, answered her sister's question:

"I never see one of those vessels without a shudder. I have an instinct which warns me that they are destined to play a dangerous, perhaps a fatal, part in the future. What is that boat doing here, in Danish waters?—I do not know. But it can be here for no good. If a war ever broke out in which we were concerned, the Sound would be our first line of defense on the west. It would be mined, by us, perhaps; if not, by our enemy. Who can tell whether that submarine has not been sent out by some Power which is already plotting against peace, to explore the bed of the strait, with a view to laying down mines hereafter?"

The other Empress listened with a grave countenance.

"I hope your fears are not well founded. I can think of no Power that is ever likely to attack you. It is my nephew, or rather those who surround him, from whom the signal for war is likely to come, if it ever does come."

The widowed Empress bowed her head.

"You know what my hopes and wishes are," she answered. "If my son listened to me there would be no fear of his departing from the peaceful ways of my dear husband. But there are secret influences always at work, as stealthy in their nature as that very craft——"

The speaker paused as she glanced 'round in search of the black streak and gray smoke-wreath which had attracted her notice a minute before. But she looked in vain.

Like a phantom the submarine had disappeared, leaving no trace of its presence.

The Empress uttered an ejaculation of dismay, which was echoed by her sister.

"Where is it now? Where did it go? Has it sunk, or has it gone back to where it came from?"

To these questions there could be no answer. The smooth waters glistened in the sunlight as merrily as if no threatening craft was gliding beneath the surface on some errand fraught with danger to the world.

"Perhaps they saw they were observed, and dived under for concealment," suggested the second Empress.

Her sister sighed gently.

"I was telling you that that submarine was a type of the secret dangers which beset us. I know, beyond all doubt, that there are men in the innermost circle of the Court, men who have my son's ear, and can do almost what they like with him, who are at heart longing for a great war, and are always working underground to bring it about. And if they succeed, and we are taken unprepared by a stronger foe, there will be a revolution which may cost my son his throne, if not his life."

There was a brief silence. Then the Empress who had listened to this declaration murmured in a low voice:

"Heaven grant that the war is not one between you and us!"

"Heaven grant it!" was the fervent reply. And then, after a moment's reflection, the widowed Empress added in an eager voice:

"But we—cannot we do something to avert such a fearful calamity?"

Her sister pressed her arm as though to assure her of sympathy.

"Yes, yes," the other continued. "We can do much if we will. Though my son does not always take my advice, he has never yet refused to listen to me. And in moments of grave stress he sometimes consults me of his own accord. And I know that you, too, have influence. Your people worship you. Your husband——"

The Western Empress interrupted gently:

"I cannot play the part that you play. I do not claim the right to be consulted, or to give direct advice. Do not ask me to step outside my sphere. I can give information; I can be a channel sometimes between your Court and ours, a channel which you can trust as I fear you cannot always trust your ministers and diplomatic agents. More than that I should not like to promise."

"But that is very much," was the grateful response. "That may be quite enough. Provided we can arrange a code by which I can always communicate with you safely and secretly, it may be possible to avert war at any time."

"What do you propose?"

"It is very simple. If any crisis comes about through no fault of my son's—if the party who are conspiring to make a war arrange some unexpected *coup* which we could not foresee or prevent—and if I am sure that my son sincerely desires peace, I can send you a message—one word will be enough—which you can take as an assurance that we mean to put ourselves right with you, and to thwart the plotters."

The Western Empress bowed her head.

"I accept the mission. And the word—what shall it be?"

The other glanced 'round the horizon once more, and then, bending her lips to her imperial sister's ear, whispered a single word.

The two great women who had just exchanged a pledge for the peace of the world were moving slowly along the terrace again, when the Western sister said, thoughtfully,

"I think I know another way to aid you."

The Eastern Empress halted, and gazed at her with eagerness.

"I know the difficulties that surround you," her sister pursued, "and that the greatest of them all is having no one in your service whom you can entirely and absolutely trust."

"That is so," was the mournful admission.

"Now I have heard of a man—I have never actually employed him myself, but I have heard of him from those who have, and they tell me he is incorruptible. In addition, he is a man who has never experienced the sensation of fear, and his abilities are so great that he has been called in to solve almost every problem of international politics that has arisen in recent years."

"But this man—how can he be obtained?"

"At present he is retained in our secret service. I must not conceal from you that he is partly a Pole by descent, and as such he has no love for your Empire. But if it were made clear to him that in serving you he was serving us, and defeating the designs of the anti-popular and despotic clique at your Court, I feel sure he would consent to place himself at your disposal."

The Eastern Empress listened intently to her sister's words. At the close she said,

"Thank you. I will try this man, if you can prevail on him to come to me. What is his name?"

"I expect you must have heard of him already, It is——"

"*Monsieur V——?*"

The second Empress nodded.

No more was said.

The two imperial figures passed away along the terrace, silhouetted against the red and stormy sunset sky, like two ministering spirits of peace brooding over a battleground of blood.

Chapter 1 The Instructions of Monsieur V— —

The great monarch by whose gracious command I write this narrative has given me his permission to preface it with the following remarkable document:

Minute: It is considered that it cannot but promote the cause of peace and good understanding between the British and Russian Governments if Monsieur V— — be authorized to relate in the columns of some publication enjoying a wide circulation, the steps by which he was enabled to throw light on the occurrences in the North Sea.

By the Cabinet.

In addition, I desire to state for the benefit of those who profess to see some impropriety in the introduction of real names into a narrative of this kind, that objections precisely similar to theirs were long ago raised, and long ago disposed of, in the case of Parliamentary reports, newspaper articles, society papers, and comic publications of all kinds; and, further, that I have never received the slightest intimation that my literary methods were displeasing to the illustrious personages whom my narratives are intended to honor.

With this apology I may be permitted to proceed.

On a certain day in the winter which preceded the outbreak of war between Russia and Japan, I received a summons to Buckingham Palace, London, to interview the Marquis of Bedale.

I am unable to fix the precise date, as I have forsworn the dangerous practice of keeping a diary ever since the head of the French police convinced me that he had deciphered a code telegram of mine to the Emperor of Morocco.

The Marquis and I were old friends, and, anticipating that I should find myself required to start immediately on some mission which might involve a long absence from my headquarters in Paris, I took my confidential secretary with me as far as the British capital, utilizing the time taken by the journey in instructing him how to deal with the various affairs I had in hand.

I had just finished explaining to him the delicate character of the negotiation then pending between the new King of Servia and Prince Ferdinand of Bulgaria, when the train rolled into Charing Cross.

Not wishing any one, however high in my confidence, to know too much of my movements, I ordered him to remain seated in the railway carriage, while I slipped out of the station and into the closed brougham for which I had telegraphed from Dover.

I had said in the wire that I wished to be driven to a hotel in Piccadilly. It was not till I found myself in Cockspur Street that I pulled the check-string, and ordered the coachman to take me to Buckingham Palace.

I mention these details in order to show that my precautions to insure secrecy are always of the most thorough character, so that, in fact, it would be quite impossible for any one to unveil my proceedings unless I voluntarily opened my lips.

The instructions which I received from Lord Bedale were brief and to the point:

"You are aware, of course, Monsieur V— —, that there is a possibility of war breaking out before long between Russia and Japan."

"It is more than a possibility, I am afraid, my lord. Things have gone so far that I do not believe it is any longer possible to avert war."

His lordship appeared gravely concerned.

"Do you tell me that it is too late for you to interfere with effect?" he demanded anxiously.

"Even for me," I replied with firmness.

Lord Bedale threw at me a glance almost imploring in its entreaty.

"If you were to receive the most ample powers, the most liberal funds; if you were to be placed in direct communication with one of the most exalted personages in the Court of St Petersburg—would it still be impossible?"

I shook my head.

"Your lordship should have sent for me a fortnight ago. We have lost twelve days, that is to say, twelve battles."

The Marquis of Bedale looked more and more distressed.

"At least you can try?" he suggested.

"I can try. But I am not omnipotent, my lord," I reminded him.

He breathed a sigh of relief before going on to say:

"But that is only the preliminary. Great Britain is bound to come to the assistance of Japan in certain contingencies."

"In the event of her being attacked by a second Power," I observed.

"Precisely. I rely on you to prevent that contingency arising."

"That is a much easier matter, I confess."

"Then you undertake to keep the war from extending to us?"

"I undertake to keep a second Power from attacking Japan," I answered cautiously.

Lord Bedale was quick to perceive my reservation.

"But in that case we cannot be involved, surely?" he objected.

"I cannot undertake to keep you from attacking Russia," I explained grimly.

"But we should not dream of attacking her—without provocation," he returned, bewildered.

"I fancy you will have a good deal of provocation," I retorted.

"Why? What makes you think that?" he demanded.

I suspected that Lord Bedale was either sounding me, or else that he had not been taken into the full confidence of those for whom he was acting.

I responded evasively:

"There are two personages in Europe, neither of whom will leave one stone unturned in the effort to involve you in war with Russia."

"And they are?"

Even as he put the question, Lord Bedale, as though acting unconsciously, raised one hand to his mustache, and gave it a pronounced upward twirl.

"I see your lordship knows one of them," I remarked. "The other——"

He bent forward eagerly.

"Yes? The other?"

"The other is a woman."

"A woman?"

He fell back in his chair in sheer surprise.

"The other," I repeated in my most serious tone, "is a woman, perhaps the most formidable woman now living, not even excepting the Dowager Empress of China."

"And her name?"

"Her name would tell you nothing."

"Still——"

"If you really wish to hear it——"

"I more than wish. I urge you."

"Her name is the Princess Y——."

Scarcely had the name of this dangerous and desperate woman passed my lips than I regretted having uttered it.

Had I foreseen the perils to which I exposed myself by that single slip I might have hesitated in going on with my enterprise.

As it was I determined to tell the Marquis of Bedale nothing more.

"This business is too urgent to admit of a moment's unnecessary delay," I declared, rising to my feet. "If your lordship has no further instructions to give me, I will leave you."

"One instant!" cried Lord Bedale. "On arriving in Petersburg you will go straight to report yourself to her majesty the Empress Dagmar."

I bowed my head to conceal the expression which might have told his lordship that I intended to do nothing of the kind.

"Your credentials," he added with a touch of theatricality, "will consist of a single word."

"And that word?" I inquired.

He handed me a sealed envelope.

"I do not myself know it. It is written on a piece of paper inside that envelope, and I have to ask you to open the envelope, read the word, and then destroy the paper in my presence."

I shrugged my shoulders as I proceeded to break the seal. But no sooner did my eyes fall on the word within, and above all on the handwriting in which that word was written, than I experienced a sensation of admiring pleasure.

"Tell the writer, if you please, my lord, that I am grateful for this mark of confidence, which I shall endeavor to deserve."

I rolled up the paper into a tiny pellet, swallowed it, and left the room and the Palace without uttering another word.

I never use the same stratagem more than once. It is to this rule that I attribute my success.

On previous missions to Russia I assumed the disguises of a French banker, of the private secretary to Prince Napoleon, of an emissary from an Indian Maharaja, and of an Abyssinian Maduga.

I now decided to go thither as an Englishman, or rather— for there is a distinction between the two—as a Little Englander.

It appeared to me that no character could be more calculated to gain me the confidence of the Anglophobes of the Russian Court. I anticipated that they would smother me with attentions, and that from their hypocritical professions I should stand a good chance of learning what was actually in their minds.

No sooner had I taken this decision, which was while the brougham was being driven along the Mall, than I gave the order "— — House."

I was driven to the office of a well known review conducted by a journalist of boundless philanthropy and credulity. Mr. Place—as I will call him—was within, and I at once came to business.

"I am a Peace Crusader," I announced. "I have devoted myself to the sacred cause of which you are the foremost champion. At present war is threatened in the Far East. I am going to Russia to persuade the war party to abandon their designs. I have come here to ask you for your aid and countenance in this pious enterprise."

The editor gave me a doubtful glance.

"If it is a question of financial aid," he said not very

encouragingly, "I must refer you to the treasurer of the World's Peace League. I am afraid our friends — —"

"No, no," I interrupted him. "It is not a question of funds. I am a wealthy man, and if you need a subscription at any time you have only to apply to me. What I desire is your moral support, your valuable advice, and perhaps a few introductions to the friends of peace in the Russian capital."

The editor's face brightened.

"Of course!" he exclaimed in cordial tones. "I will support you with all my heart. I will write up your mission in the *Review*, and I will give you as many introductions as you need. What is your name, again?"

"Sterling. Mr. Melchisadek Sterling."

The philanthropist nodded and touched a bell on his table.

"I will give you a letter," he said, as his secretary came in and seated herself at the typewriter, "to the noblest creature I have ever met, a woman of high birth and immense fortune who has devoted herself to the cause."

And turning 'round in his chair he dictated to the attentive secretary:

"*My dear Princess Y — —*"

It needed all that command over my features which it has taken me twenty years to acquire to conceal the emotion with which I heard this name. Less than half an hour had passed since I had warned Lord Bedale that the Princess would be the most formidable enemy in my path, and now, on the very threshold of my enterprise, her name confronted me like an omen.

I need not repeat the highly colored phrases in which the unsuspecting philanthropist commended me to this artful and formidable woman as a fellow-worker in the holy cause of human brotherhood.

Not content with this service, the editor wanted to arrange a meeting of his league or brotherhood, or whatever it was, to give me a public send-off. As I understood that the meeting would partake of a religious character I could not bring myself to accept the offer.

In addition to the letter to the Princess Y— —, he gave me another to a member of the staff of the Russian Embassy in London, a M. Gudonov. He also urged me to call upon a member of Parliament, a rising politician who is not unlikely to have a ministerial post in the next government, and who has made himself known as an apologist of the Czar's. But as I had good reason to know that this gentleman was by no means a disinterested dupe, like Mr. Place, I prudently left him alone.

On going to the Russian Embassy to have my passport viséd I inquired for M. Gudonov.

The moment he entered the room I recognized him as one of the most unscrupulous agents of the notorious Third Section, one of the gang who drugged and kidnapped poor Alexander of Bulgaria. My own disguise, it is hardly necessary to say, was impenetrable.

This precious apostle of peace greeted me with unction, on the editor's introduction.

"You are going to our country on a truly noble errand," he declared, with tears in his eyes. "We Russians have reason to feel grateful to worthy Englishmen like you, who can rise above national prejudices and do justice to the benevolent designs of the Czar and his advisers."

"I hope that I may be instrumental in averting a great

catastrophe," I said piously.

"Even if you fail in preventing war," the Russian replied, "you will be able to tell your countrymen when you return, that it was due to the insane ambition of the heathen Japanese. It is the 'Yellow Peril,' my friend, to which that good Emperor William has drawn attention, from which we are trying to save Europe."

I nodded my head as if well satisfied.

"Whatever you and your friends in Petersburg tell me, I shall believe," I assured him. "I am convinced of the good intention of your Government."

The Russian fairly grinned at this simplicity.

"You cannot find a more trustworthy informant than the Princess Y— —," he said gravely. "And just now she is in a position to know a very great deal."

"How so?" I asked naturally—not that I doubted the statement.

"The Princess has just been appointed a lady-in-waiting to her imperial majesty the Dowager Empress Dagmar."

This was a serious blow. Knowing what I did of the past of Princess Y— —, I felt that no ordinary pressure must have been brought to bear to secure her admission into the household of the Czaritza. And with what motive? It was a question to which there could be only one answer. The War Party had guessed or suspected that the Czar's mother was opposed to them, and they had resolved to place a spy on her actions.

Inwardly thankful to Mr. Place for having been the means of procuring me this important information in advance, I received my passport and quitted the Embassy with the heartfelt congratulations of the ex-kidnapper.

Forty-eight hours later I had crossed the Russian frontier, and my life was in the hands of the Princess.

My first step on arriving in the capital of the North was to put up at the favorite hotel of English visitors. The coupons of a celebrated tourist agency were credentials in themselves, and I had not forgotten to provide myself with the three articles indispensable to the outfit of every traveling Briton—a guide book, a prayer book, and a bath sponge.

At the risk of incurring the suspicions of the police agent stationed in the hotel, I mingled some hot water in the bath which I took on the first morning after my arrival. Then, having made my toilet and eaten the heavy breakfast provided for English visitors, I set out, suffering sadly from indigestion, to present my letter of introduction to the Princess.

As this woman, the most brilliant recruit ever received into the Russian secret service, and a foe of whom I am not ashamed to confess that I felt some fear, has never been heard of by the public of Great Britain, I shall say a word concerning her.

The Princess, whose Christian name was Sophia, was the daughter of a boyar of Little Russia. Her extraordinary beauty, while she was still a very young girl, attracted the attention of the governor of the province, Prince Y——, who was one of the wealthiest nobles in the Empire, and a widower. He made proposals for her hand which were accepted by her father, without the girl herself being asked to express an opinion in the matter, and at the age when an English girl would be leaving home for a convent or "high-school," Sophia became the Governor's wife.

Almost immediately the Prince resigned his government and went to live in his splendid palace on the Nevsky Prospect, in Petersburg. Before very long, society in the Russian capital was startled to hear of the sudden deaths in rapid succession of both the Prince's children by his former wife, a son and a daughter. Then, after a brief interval, followed the tragic death of the Prince himself, who was found in bed one morning by his valet, with his throat cut.

The almost satanic beauty and fascination of the youthful Princess had made her from the very first one of the most conspicuous personages at the Imperial Court. These three deaths, following on the heels of one another, roused the most dreadful suspicions, and the Czar Alexander III. personally charged his minister of justice to see that the law was carried out.

Accordingly the police took possession of the palace while the corpse of its late owner still lay where it had been found. The most searching investigations were made, the servants were questioned and threatened, and it was rumored that the widow herself was for a short time under arrest.

Suddenly a great change took place. The police withdrew, professing themselves satisfied that no crime had been committed. The deaths of the son and daughter were put down to natural causes, and that of the Prince was pronounced a suicide, due to grief at the loss of his children. Some of the servants disappeared—it was said into Siberia—and in due course the Princess resumed her place in society and at Court, as though nothing were amiss.

Nevertheless, from that hour, as I have every reason to know, her life was really that of a slave to the head of the secret police. She appeared to go about unfettered, and to revel in the enjoyment of every luxury; but her time, her actions, and the vast wealth bequeathed to her by her husband, were all at the disposal of her tyrant.

Time after time, in half the capitals of Europe, but more especially, of course, in that of Russia, I had come on traces of this terrible woman, not less terrible if it were true that she was herself the most miserable victim of the system of which she formed part.

But singularly enough, though I had heard so much of the Princess I had never actually found myself pitted against her. And, more singularly still, I had never met her.

From this it will be gathered that I experienced a sensation of more than ordinary curiosity and even apprehension as I presented myself at the house in the Nevsky Prospect, and asked to be admitted to the presence of its mistress.

"Her highness is on duty at the Palace to-day," I was told by the chamberlain who received me in the inner hall. "Her carriage is just ordered to take her there. However, I will take up your letter, and inquire when her highness can see you."

I sat down in the hall, outwardly a calm, stolid Briton, but inwardly a wrestler, wound up to the highest pitch of excitement and impatient for the sight of his antagonist.

To pass the time suitably, I took my guide-book out of my pocket and began to read. The book opened at Herr Baedaker's description of the gloomy fortress of the Schlüsselburg, the dreaded prison of the foes of the Czar.

The description did not tend to soothe my nerves, conscious as I was that the woman I was about to meet could consign me to the most noisome dungeon in the fortress by merely lifting her little finger.

I was just closing the book with an involuntary shudder when I heard a light, almost girlish, laugh from above. I looked hastily, and saw the woman I had come to measure myself against standing poised like a bird on the top of the grand staircase.

As I rose hurriedly to my feet, taking in every detail of her superb yet delicate figure, her complexion like a blush-rose, her lustrous eyes—they were dark violet on a closer view—and the cloud of rippling gold that framed her brow, I was moved, yes, positively carried away for a moment, by a sentiment such as few women have been able to inspire in me.

Perceiving, no doubt, that she had produced the desired impression, the Princess ran lightly down the stairs and came toward me holding out two tiny hands, the fingers of which were literally gloved in diamonds.

"My friend! My noble Englishman!" she exclaimed in the purest French. "And since when have you known that dear Monsieur Place?"

I checked myself on the point of replying, pretended to falter, and then muttered in the worst French I could devise on the spur of the moment:

"*Parlez-vous Anglais, s'il vous plaît, Madame?*"

The Princess shook her head reproachfully.

"You speak French too well not to understand it, I suspect," she retorted in the same language. Then dropping it for English, marred only by a slight Slavonic accent, she repeated:

"But tell me,—dear Mr. Place, he is a great friend of yours, I suppose?"

"I can hardly claim the honor of his personal friendship," I replied, rather lamely. "But I have always known and admired him as a public man."

"Ah! He is so good, is he not? So generous, so confiding,

so great a friend of our dear Russia. You know Mr. — —?"

The name she uttered was that of the politician referred to above. She slipped it out swiftly, with the action of a cat pouncing.

I shook my head with an air of distress.

"I am afraid I am not important enough to know such a great man as that," I said with affected humility.

The Princess hastened to relieve my embarrassment.

"What is that to us!" she exclaimed. "You are an Englishman, you are benevolent, upright, truthful, and you esteem our country. Such men are always welcome in Russia. The Czaritza is waiting for me; but you will come back and dine with me, if not to-night, then to-morrow, or the next day. I will send an invitation to your hotel. My friends shall call on you. You are staying at the— —?"

I mentioned the name of the hotel, murmuring my thanks.

"That is nothing," the beautiful woman went on in the same eager strain. "I shall have good news for you when we meet again, believe me. Yes—" she lowered her voice almost to a whisper—"our dear Czar is going to take the negotiations into his own hands. So it is said. His majesty is determined to preserve peace. The odious intrigues of the War group will be defeated, I can assure you. You will not be disappointed, my dear Mr.— —" she snatched the editor's letter from her muff and glanced at it—"Mr. Sterling, if I tell you that you are going to have your journey for nothing. You will have a good time in Petersburg, all the same. But believe me when I tell you so, your journey will fortunately be for nothing!"

And with the repetition of these words, and another

bright bow and look which dazzled my senses, the wonderful creature swept past me to where the chamberlain stood ready to hand her into her carriage.

For nothing?

Chapter 3 *The Head of the Manchurian Syndicate*

No reader can have failed to notice one remarkable point in the interview between the Princess Y—— and myself. I refer of course to her invitation to me to dine with her in the course of a day or two.

Unless the etiquette of the Russian Court differed greatly from that of most others in Europe, it would be most indecorous for a lady-in-waiting, during her turn of service, to give entertainments at her private house.

I felt certain that this invitation concealed some trap, but I puzzled myself uselessly in trying to guess what it could be.

In the meantime I did not neglect certain other friends of mine in the city on the Neva, from whom I had some hope of receiving assistance.

Although I have never gone so far as to enroll myself as an active Nihilist, I am what is known as an Auxiliary. In other words, without being under the orders of the great secret committee which wages underground war with the Russian Government, I have sometimes rendered it voluntary services, and I have at all times the privilege of communicating with it, and exchanging information.

While waiting for the next move on the part of the Princess, therefore, I decided to get in touch with the revolutionists.

I made my way on foot to a certain tavern situated near the port, and chiefly patronized by German and Scandinavian sailors.

The host of the Angel Gabriel, as the house was called, was a Nihilist of old standing, and one of their most useful agents for introducing forbidden literature into the empire.

Printed mostly in London, in a suburb called Walworth, the revolutionary tracts are shipped to Bergen or Lubeck, and brought thence by these sailors concealed in their bedding. At night, after the customs officers have departed, a boat with a false keel puts off from a quay higher up the Neva, and passes down the river to where the newly arrived ship is lying; the packages are dropped overboard as it drifts past the side and hidden under the bottom boards; and then the boat returns up the river, where its cargo is transferred to the cellars of the tavern.

The host, a namesake of the Viceroy of Manchuria, was serving in the bar when I came in. I called for a glass of vodka, and in doing so made the sign announcing myself as an Auxiliary.

Alexieff said nothing in reply, but the sailors lounging in the bar began to finish off their drinks and saunter out one by one, till in a short time the place was empty.

"Well?" said the tavern-keeper, as soon as we were alone.

It was not my first visit to the Angel Gabriel, and I lost no time in convincing Alexieff of my identity. As soon as he recognized me, I said:—

"You know the Princess Y——?"

The expression of rage and fear which convulsed his features was a sufficient answer.

"You know, moreover, that she is at present working her hardest to bring about a war between Russia and Japan, with the hope of ultimately involving Great Britain?"

He nodded sullenly.

"How does that affect your friends?" I asked cautiously. Something in the man's face warned me not to show my own hand just then.

"We hate her, of course," he said grudgingly, "but just now we have received orders that she is not to be interfered with."

I drew a deep breath.

"Then you regard this war — — ?"

"We regard it as the beginning of the revolution," he answered. "We know that the Empire is utterly unprepared. The Viceroy Alexieff is a vain boaster. Port Arthur is not provisioned. The Navy is rotten. The Army cannot be recruited except by force. The taxes are already excessive and cannot be increased. In short, we look forward to see the autocracy humiliated. The moment its prestige is gone, and the moujik feels the pinch of famine, our chance will come."

I saw that I had come to the wrong quarter for assistance.

"Then you will do nothing against this woman at present?" I remarked, anxious to leave the impression that she was the only object of my concern.

"No. At least not until war is definitely declared. After that I cannot say."

"And you think the war sure to come?"

"We are certain of it. One of our most trusted members is on the board of the Manchurian Syndicate."

"The Syndicate which has obtained the concessions in Korea?"

"Against which Japan has protested, yes."

I felt the full force of this announcement, having watched the proceedings of the Syndicate for some months for reasons of my own.

Every student of modern history has remarked the fact that all recent wars have been promoted by great combinations of capitalists. The causes which formerly led to war between nation and nation have ceased to operate. Causes, or at least pretexts, for war continue to occur, but whether they are followed up depends mainly on commercial considerations. A distant Government is oppressing its subjects, it may be in Turkey, it may be in Cuba, it may be in Africa. No matter, some great Power suddenly discovers it is interested; the drums are beaten, the flag is unfurled, and armies are launched on their path. The next year, perhaps, the same Power sees its own subjects massacred wantonly off its own coasts by a foreign fleet. Nothing happens; a few speeches are made, and the whole incident is referred to arbitration, and forgotten.

It is the consideration of money which decides between peace and war.

Perceiving it was useless to ask any assistance of the Nihilists in my forlorn enterprise, I returned sadly to my hotel.

Hardly had I finished the immense lunch on which I was compelled to gorge myself, when a waiter brought me a card, the name on which gave me an electric shock.

"*M. Petrovitch.*"

Every one has heard of this man, the promoter of the Manchurian Syndicate, and, if report spoke truly, the possessor of an influence over the young Czar which could be attributed only to some occult art.

I could not doubt that this powerful personage had been instigated to call on me by the Princess Y— —.

What then? Was it likely that she would have sent the most influential man in the imperial circle to wait upon a traveling fanatic, a visionary humanitarian from Exeter Hall?

Impossible! Somehow something must have leaked out to

rouse the suspicions of this astute plotter, and make her guess that I was not what I seemed.

It was with the sensations of a man struggling in the meshes of an invisible net that I saw M. Petrovitch enter the room.

The celebrated wire-puller, whose name was familiar to every statesman and stock-broker in Europe, had an appearance very unlike his reputation.

He was the court dandy personified. Every detail of his dress was elaborated to the point of effeminacy. His hands were like a girl's, his long hair was curled and scented, he walked with a limp and spoke with a lisp, removing a gold-tipped cigarette from his well-displayed teeth.

As the smoke of the cigarette drifted toward me, I was conscious of an acute, but imperfect, twinge of memory. The sense of smell, though the most neglected, is the most reliable sense with which we are furnished. I could not be mistaken in thinking I had smelt tobacco like that before.

"I have come to see you without losing a moment, Mr. Sterling," he said in very good English. "My good friend Madame Y— — sent me a note from the Palace to beg me to show you every attention. It is too bad that an ambassador of peace—a friend of that great and good man, Place, should be staying in a hotel, while hundreds of Russians would be delighted to welcome him as their guest. My house is a poor one, it is true, and I am hardly of high enough rank, still— —"

The intriguer was asking me to transfer myself to his roof, to become his prisoner, in effect.

"I cannot thank you enough," I responded, "but I am not going to stay. The Princess has convinced me that the war-cloud will blow over, and I think of going on to Constantinople to intercede with the Sultan on behalf of the Armenians."

"A noble idea," M. Petrovitch responded warmly. "What would the world do without such men as you? But at all events you will dine with me before you go?"

It was the second invitation to dinner I had received that day. But, after all, I could hardly suspect a trap in everything.

"Do you share the hopes of the Princess?" I asked M. Petrovitch, after thanking him for his hospitality.

The syndicate-monger nodded.

"I have been working night and day for peace," he declared impudently, "and I think I may claim that I have done some good. The Japanese are seeking for an excuse to attack us, but they will not get it."

"The Manchurian Syndicate?" I ventured to hint, rising to go to the bell.

"The Syndicate is wholly in favor of peace," he assured me, watching my movement with evident curiosity. "We require it, in fact, to develop our mines, our timber concessions, our ——"

A waiter entered in response to my ring.

"Bring me some cigarettes—your best," I ordered him.

As the man retreated it was borne in on my guest that he had been guilty of smoking in my room without offering me his case.

"A thousand pardons!" he exclaimed. "Won't you try one of mine?"

I took a cigarette from the case he held out, turned it between my fingers, and lit it from the end farthest from the maker's imprint.

"If I am satisfied that all danger is removed I should be inclined to apply for some shares in your undertaking," I said, giving the promoter a meaning look.

From the expression in his eyes it was evident that this precious scoundrel was ready to sell Czar, Russia and fellow-promoters all together.

While he was struggling between his natural greed and his suspicion the waiter reentered with some boxes of cigarettes.

I smelt the tobacco of each and made my choice, at the same time pitching the half-smoked cigarette given to me by M. Petrovitch into the fireplace, among the ashes.

"Your tobacco is a little too strong for me," I remarked by way of excuse.

But the Russian was wrapped up in the thought of the bribe at which I had just hinted.

"I shall bear in mind what you say," he declared, as he rose.

"Depend upon it, if it is possible for me to meet your wishes, I shall be happy to do so."

I saw him go off, like a fish with the bait in its mouth. Directly the door closed behind him I sprang to the fireplace, rescued the still burning cigarette and quenched it, and then, carefully brushing away the dust, read the maker's brand once more.

An hour later simultaneous messages were speeding over the wires to my correspondents in London, Amsterdam and Hamburg:

Ascertain what becomes of all cigarettes made by Gregorides; brand, Crown Aa.

The next morning at breakfast I found the two invitations already promised. That of the head of the Manchurian Syndicate was for the same night.

Resolved not to remain in the dark any longer as to the reason for this apparent breach of etiquette, I decided to do what the Marquis of Bedale had suggested, namely, approach the Dowager Empress in person.

Well accustomed to the obstacles which beset access to royalty, I drove to the Palace in a richly appointed carriage from the best livery stable in Petersburg, and sent in my card to the chamberlain by an equerry.

"I have a message to the Czaritza which I am instructed to give to her majesty in person," I told him. "Be good enough to let her know that the messenger from the Queen of England has arrived."

He went out of the room, and at the end of ten minutes the door opened again and admitted — the Princess Y — — !

Overpowered by this unlucky accident, as I at first supposed it to be, I rose to my feet, muttering some vague phrase of courtesy.

But the Princess soon showed me that the meeting did not take her by surprise.

"So you have a message for my dear mistress?" she cried in an accent of gay reproach. "And you never breathed a word of it to me. Mr. Sterling, I shall begin to think you are a conspirator. *How* long did you say you had known that good Mr. Place? But I am talking while her majesty is waiting. Have you any password by which the Czaritza will know whom you come from?"

"I can tell that only to her majesty, I am afraid," I answered guardedly.

"I am in her majesty's confidence."

And bringing her exquisite face so near to mine that I was oppressed by the scent of the tuberoses in her bosom, she whispered three syllables in my ear.

Dismayed by this proof of the fatal progress the dangerous police agent had already made, I could only admit by a silent bow that the password was correct.

"Then come with me, Mr. Sterling," the Princess said with what sounded like a malicious accent on the name.

The reception which I met from the Dowager Empress was gracious in the extreme. I need not recount all that passed. Her imperial majesty repeated with evident sincerity the assurances which had already been given me in a different spirit by the two arch-intriguers.

"There will be no war. The Czar has personally intervened. He has taken the negotiations out of the hands of Count Lamsdorff, and written an autograph letter to the Mikado which will put an end to the crisis."

I listened with a distrust which I could not wholly conceal.

"I trust his majesty has not intervened too late," I said respectfully, my mind bent on framing some excuse to get rid of the listener. "According to the newspapers the patience of the Japanese is nearly exhausted."

"No more time will be lost," the Czaritza responded. "The messenger leaves Petersburg to-night with the Czar's letter."

I stole a cautious glance in the direction of the Princess Y
——. She was breathing deeply, her eyes fixed on the Czaritza's
lips, and her hands tightly clenched.

I put on an air of great relief.

"In that case, your majesty, I have no more to do in
Petersburg. I will wire the good news to Lord Bedale, and return
to England to-morrow or the next day. I beg your pardon,
Princess!" I pretended to exclaim by a sudden afterthought,
"*after* the next day." And turning once more to the mother of the
Czar, I explained:

"The Princess has honored me with an invitation to
dinner."

The Dowager Empress glanced at her attendant in evident
surprise.

"I must implore your pardon, Madam," the Princess
stammered, in real confusion. "I am aware I ought to have
solicited your leave in the first place, but knowing that this
gentleman came from——"

She broke off, fairly unable to meet the questioning gaze
of her imperial mistress.

I pretended to come to her relief.

"I have a private message," I said to the Empress.

"You may leave us, Princess," the Empress said coldly.

As soon as the door had closed on her, I gave a warning
look at the Czaritza.

"That woman, Madam, is the most dangerous agent in the
secret service of your Empire."

I trusted to the little scene I had just contrived to prepare
the mind of the Czaritza for this intimation. But she received it
as a matter of course.

"Sophia Y— — has been all that you say, Monsieur V— —. I am well acquainted with her history. The poor thing has been a victim of the most fiendish cruelty on the part of the Minister of Police, for years. At last, unable to bear her position any longer, she appealed to me. She told me her harrowing story, and implored me to receive her, and secure her admission to a convent. I investigated the case thoroughly."

"Your majesty will pardon me, I am sure, if I say that as a man with some experience of intrigue, I thoroughly distrust that woman's sincerity. She is intimate with M. Petrovitch, to my knowledge."

"But M. Petrovitch is also on the side of peace, so I am assured."

I began to despair.

"You will believe me, or disbelieve me as your majesty pleases. But I am accustomed to work for those who honor me with their entire confidence. If the Princess Y— — is to be taken into the secret of my work on your majesty's behalf, I must respectfully ask to be released."

As I offered her majesty this alternative in a firm voice, I was inwardly trembling. On the reply hung, perhaps, the fate of two continents.

But the Dowager Empress did not hesitate.

"What you stipulate for shall be done, Monsieur V— —. I am too well aware of the value of your services, and the claims you have on the confidence of your employers, to dispute your conditions."

"The messenger who is starting to-night—does the Princess know who he is?"

"I believe so. It is no secret. The messenger is Colonel

Menken."

"In that case he will never reach Tokio."

Her majesty could not suppress a look of horror.

"What do you advise?" she demanded tremulously.

"His majesty the Czar must at once write a duplicate of the despatch, unknown to any living soul but your majesty, and that despatch must be placed by you in my hands."

The Dowager Empress gazed at me for a moment in consternation.

But the soundness of the plan I had proposed quickly made itself manifest to her.

"You are right, Monsieur V——," her majesty said approvingly. "I will communicate with the Czar without delay. By what time do you want the despatch?"

"In time to catch the Siberian express to-night, if your majesty pleases. I purpose to travel by the same train as Colonel Menken—it is possible I may be able to avert a tragedy.

"And since your majesty has told me that the Princess Y —— is aware of the Colonel's errand, let me venture to urge you most strongly not to let her out of your sight on any pretense until he is safely on his way."

I need not go into the details of the further arrangements made with a view to my receiving the duplicate despatch in secrecy.

I came away from the Palace fully realizing the serious nature of my undertaking. I understood now all that had worried me in the proceedings of the Princess. It was clear to me that Lord Bedale, or the personage on whose behalf he instructed me, had wired to the Dowager Empress, notifying her majesty of my coming, and that she had shown the message to her lady-in-waiting.

Blaming myself bitterly for not having impressed the necessity for caution on the Marquis, I at once set about providing myself with a more effectual disguise.

It is a proverb on the lips of every moujik in Petersburg that all Russia obeys the Czar, and the Czar obeys the Tchin. Ever since the bureaucracy deliberately allowed Alexander II. to be assassinated by the Nihilists out of anger at his reforming tendencies, the Russian monarchs have felt more real dread of their own police than of the revolutionists. The *Tchin*, the universally-pervading body of officials, who run the autocracy to fill their pockets, and indulge their vile propensities at the expense of the governed, is as omnipotent as it is corrupt. Everywhere in that vast Empire the word of the Tchinovink is law — and there is no other law except his word.

Taking the bull by the horns, I went straight to the Central Police Bureau of the capital, and asked to see a certain superintendent named Rostoy.

To this man, with whom I had had some dealings on a previous occasion, and whose character was well understood by me, I explained that I had accepted a mission from a friendly Power to travel along the Siberian Railway and report on its capacity to keep the Army of Manchuria supplied with food and ammunition in the event of war.

He expressed no surprise when I told him it was essential that I should leave Petersburg that night, and accordingly it did not take us long to come to terms.

The service which I required of him was, of course, a fresh passport, with a complete disguise which would enable me to pass anywhere along the railway or in Manchuria without being detected or interfered with by the agents of the Government.

After some discussion we decided that the safest plan would be for me to travel in the character of a Russian police officer charged with the detection of the train thieves and card-sharpers who abound on every great route of travel. I could think of no part which would serve better to enable me to watch over the safety of the Czar's envoy without exciting suspicion.

I placed in Rostoy's hands the first instalment of a heavy bribe, and arranged to return an hour before the departure of the Moscow express to carry out my transformation.

It was only as I left his office that I remembered my unlucky engagement to dine that very night with the head of the Manchurian Syndicate.

I perceived that these hospitalities were well devised checks on my movements, and it was with something of a shock that I realized that when I went to dinner that evening with the most active promoter of the war I should be carrying the Czar's peace despatch in my pocket!

If the enemies of peace had foreseen every step that I was to take in the discharge of my mission, their measures could not have been more skilfully arranged.

And as this reflection occurred to me I turned my head nervously, and remarked a man dressed like a hotel porter lounging carelessly in my track.

Chapter 5 A Dinner With the Enemy

Readers of that prince of romancers, Poe, will recollect a celebrated story in which he describes the device employed by a man of uncommon shrewdness to conceal a stolen letter from the perquisitions of the police, and the elaborate argument by which the writer proves that the highest art of concealment is to thrust the object to be hidden under the very nose of the searcher.

But that argument is one of the many mystifications in which the weird genius of Poe delighted. It is easy to see, in short, that the theory was invented to suit the story, and not the story to suit the theory. I now had before me the practical problem of concealing a document of surpassing importance, from enemies who were already on my scent, and keeping it concealed during a journey of some thousands of miles.

The ordinary hiding-places of valuable papers, such as the lining of clothes, or a false bottom to a trunk, I dismissed without serious consideration. My luggage would probably be stolen, and I might be drugged long before I reached Dalny.

The problem was all the more difficult for me because I have generally made it a rule to avoid charging myself with written instructions. I am sufficiently well known by reputation to most European sovereigns to be able to dispense with ordinary credentials. But in approaching the Mikado of Japan, a ruler to whom I was personally unknown, it was clearly necessary for me to have something in writing from the Russian Emperor.

All at once an idea flashed on my mind, so simple, and yet so incapable of detection (as it seemed to me), that I almost smiled in the face of the man who was dogging my steps along the street, no doubt under instructions from the War Syndicate.

That afternoon I was closeted with the Emperor of All the Russias in his private cabinet for nearly an hour.

It is not my habit to repeat details of private conversations, when they are not required to illustrate the progress of public events, and therefore I will say merely that the Czar was evidently in earnest in his desire to avoid war, but greatly hampered and bewildered by the difficult representations made to him by, or on behalf of, those to whose interests war was essential.

It was melancholy to see the destinies of half Europe and Asia, and the lives of scores of thousands of brave men, hanging on the will of an irresolute young man, depressed by the consciousness of his own infirmity, and desperately seeking for some stronger mind on which to lean. Had I not been placed by my Polish sentiment in a position of antagonism to the Czardom, perhaps—but it is useless to indulge in these reflections.

One thing in the course of the interview struck me as having great significance for the future. I found that his majesty, who had entertained at one time a strong dislike of the German Emperor, a dislike not untinged with jealousy, had now completely altered his opinion. He spoke to me of Wilhelm II. in terms of highest praise, declared that he was under the greatest obligations to him for useful warnings and advice, said that he believed he had no truer or more zealous friend.

When I drove to the house of M. Petrovitch that evening I carried, carefully sewn between the inner and outer folds of my well-starched shirt-front, where no sound of crackling would excite remark, a sheet of thin note-paper covered in a very small handwriting with the text of the Czar's letter to the ruler of Japan.

M. Petrovitch was not alone. Around his hospitable board he had gathered some of the highest and proudest personages of the Russian Court, including the Grand Duke Staniolanus, generally believed to be the heart and soul of the War Party. His imperial highness was well-known to be a desperate gambler, up to the neck in debts contracted at the card-table, and bent on recouping himself out of the wealth of Korea and Manchuria.

I was duly presented to this royal personage (whom I had met once before under widely different circumstances) in the character of a Peace Crusader, an emissary of the philanthropists of Great Britain.

At the dinner-table, where I found myself placed on my host's left hand, while the Grand Duke was on his right, the conversation continued to be in the same strain. That Petrovitch believed me to be an English peace fanatic I did not believe any longer, but I could not tell if any, or how many, of the others were in his confidence.

As soon as the solid part of the feast was disposed of, Petrovitch rose to his feet, and after a bow to the Grand Duke, launched out into a formal speech proposing my health.

He commenced with the usual professions in favor of peace, spoke of the desire felt by all Russians to preserve the friendship of England, eulogized the work done by my friend the editor, and by other less disinterested friends of Russia in London, and wound up by asking all the company to give me a cordial welcome, and to send a message of congratulation and good-will to the British public.

Knowing as I did, that the man was a consummate rogue,

who had probably invited me to his house in order to keep me under observation, and possibly to prevent my getting scent of the intrigues pursued by his friend and ally, Princess Y— —, I was still at a loss to understand the reason for this performance.

I have learned since that an account of the proceedings, with abstracts from this hypocritical speech, was telegraphed to England, and actually found its way into some of the newspapers under the heading, "Peace Demonstration in St. Petersburg: No Russian Wants War."

There was one of the guests, however, who made no pretense of listening with pleasure to the smooth speech of M. Petrovitch. This was a dark young man of about thirty, in a naval uniform. He sat scowling while his host spoke, and barely lifted his glass from the table at the conclusion.

A minute or two later I took an opportunity to ask the promoter the name of this ungracious officer.

"That?" my host exclaimed, looking 'round the table, "Oh, that is Captain Vassileffsky, one of our most distinguished sailors. He is a naval aide-de-camp to the Czar."

I made a note of his name and face, being warned by a presentiment which I could not resist that I should come across him again.

The champagne now began to flow freely, and as it flowed the tongues of many of the company were unloosed by degrees. From the subject of peace the conversation passed rapidly to the possibilities of war, and the Japanese were spoken of in a way that plainly showed me how little those present understood the resolution and resources of the Island Empire.

"The Japanese dare not fire the first shot and, since we will not, there will be no war," declared my left-hand neighbor.

"The war will be fought in Japan, not in Manchuria," affirmed the Grand Duke with a condescending air. "It will be a case of the Boers over again. They may give us some trouble, but we shall annex their country."

M. Petrovitch gave me a glance of alarm.

"Russia does not wish to add to her territory," he put in; "but we may find it necessary to leave a few troops in Tokio to maintain order, while we pursue our civilizing mission."

I need not recount the other remarks, equally arrogant.

Abstemious by habit, I had a particular reason for refraining from taking much wine on this night. It was already past nine o'clock, the train for Moscow, which connected there with the Siberian express, started at midnight, and I had to be at the police bureau by eleven at the latest to make the changes necessary for my disguise.

I therefore allowed my glass to remain full, merely touching it with my lips occasionally when my host pressed me to drink. M. Petrovitch did not openly notice my abstinence, but presently I heard him give an order to the butler who waited behind his chair.

The butler turned to the sideboard for a moment, and then came forward bearing a silver tray on which stood a flagon of cut-glass and silver with a number of exquisite little silver cups like egg-shells.

"You will not refuse to taste our Russian national beverage, Mr. Sterling," the head of the War Syndicate said persuasively, as the butler began filling the tiny cups.

It was a challenge which I could not refuse without rudeness, though it struck me as rather out of place that the vodka should be offered to me before to the imperial guest on my host's right.

The butler filled two cups, M. Petrovitch taking the second from the tray as I lifted the first to my lips.

"You know our custom," the financier exclaimed smilingly. "No heeltaps!"

He lifted his own cup with a brave air, and I tossed off the contents of my own without stopping.

As the fiery liquor ran down my throat I was conscious of something in its taste which was unlike the flavor of any vodka I had ever drunk before. But this circumstance aroused no suspicion in my mind. I confess that it never occurred to me that any one could be daring enough to employ so crude and dangerous a device as a drugged draft at a quasi-public banquet, given to an English peace emissary, with a member of the imperial family sitting at the board.

I was undeceived the next moment. Petrovitch, as soon as he saw that my cup had been emptied, sat down his own untasted, and, with a well-acted movement of surprise and regret, turned to the Grand Duke.

"I implore your pardon, sir. I did not ask if you would not honor me by taking the first cup!"

The Grand Duke, whom I readily acquitted of any share in the other's design, shrugged his shoulders with an indifferent air.

"If you wish your friends to drink vodka, you should not put champagne like this before us," he said laughing.

Petrovitch said something in reply; he turned and scolded the butler as well, I fancy. But my brain was becoming confused. I had just sufficient command of my faculties left to feign ignorance of the true situation.

"I am feeling a little faint. That *pâté*"—I contrived to murmur.

And then I heard Captain Vassileffsky cry out in an alarm that was unmistakably genuine—"Look out for the Englishman! He is swooning"—and I knew no more.

Chapter 6 *Drugged and Kidnapped*

My first thought, as my senses began to come back to me, was of the train which was due to leave Petersburg for Moscow at midnight.

I clutched at my watch, and drew it forth. The hands marked the time as 9.25. Apparently I had not been unconscious for more than a few seconds.

My second glance assured me that my clothes were not disarranged. My shirt-front, concealing the Czar's autograph letter, was exactly as when I sat down to the table.

Only after satisfying myself on these two points did I begin to take in the rest of my surroundings.

I was resting on a couch against the wall in the room where we had dined. My host, the head of the Manchuria Syndicate, was standing beside me, watching my recovery with a friendly and relieved expression, as though honestly glad to see me myself again. A servant, holding in his hand a bottle which appeared to contain sal volatile, was looking on from the foot of the bed, in an attitude of sympathetic attention. The other guests had left the room, and the state of the table, covered with half-filled glasses and hastily thrown down napkins, made it evident that they had cleared out of the way to give me a chance to come to.

The cold air blowing over my forehead told me that a window had been opened. A Russian January is not favorable to much ventilation. As a rule the houses of the well-to-do are provided with double windows, which are kept hermetically sealed while the rooms are in use. The fact that the dining-room was still warm was sufficient proof that the window could not have been opened for more than the briefest time.

It was a singular thing that, in spite of these assurances that my swoon had been an affair of moments only, I was seized by an overmastering desire to get away from the house immediately.

I heard M. Petrovitch exclaim—

"Thank Heaven—you are better! I began to be afraid that your seizure was going to last. I must go and reassure my guests. The Grand Duke will be delighted to hear your are recovering. He was most distressed at the attack."

I sat upright with an effort, and staggered to my feet.

"I am ashamed to have given you so much trouble," I said. "I can't remember ever fainting like this before. Please make my excuses to his imperial highness and the rest of the company."

"But what are you doing?" cried M. Petrovitch in dismay. "You must not attempt to move yet."

"I shall be better in bed," I answered in a voice which I purposely strove to render as faint as possible. "If you will excuse me, I will go straight to my hotel."

The promoter's brow wrinkled. I saw that he was trying to devise some pretext to detain me, and my anxiety to find myself clear of his house redoubled.

"If you will do me a favor, I should be glad if you would let one of your servants come with me as far as the hotel," I said. "I am feeling rather giddy and weak."

The secret chief of the War Party caught eagerly at the suggestion. It was no doubt exactly what he desired.

"Mishka," he said, turning to the servant, and speaking in Russian, "this gentleman asks you to accompany him to his hotel, as he has not yet recovered. Take great care of him, and do not leave him until he is safe in his own bed."

The man nodded, giving his master a look which said—I understand what you want me to do.

Thanks to this request on my part, M. Petrovitch raised no further objection to my departure. I stumbled out of the room, pretending to cling to the servant's arm for support, and let him help me on with my furs, while the porter was summoning a sleigh.

There was a hurried consultation in low tones between my host and the porter. Rather to my surprise the carriage, when it appeared, was a closed one, being a species of brougham on runners instead of wheels. I allowed myself to be carried down the steps like a child, and placed inside; the door was closed, with the windows carefully drawn up, and the jailer—for such he was to all intents and purposes—got on the box.

The sleigh swept out of the courtyard and across the city. Directly it was in the street, I very softly lowered one of the windows and peered out. The streets seemed to me more deserted than usual at such an hour. I was idly wondering whether the imminence of war could account for this when I heard a church clock beginning to strike.

Once—twice—the chimes rang out. And then, as I was preparing to close the window, they went on a third time—a fourth!

I held my breath, and listened with straining ears, as the great notes boomed forth from the distant town across the silent streets and houses.

One—two—three—four—five—six—seven—eight—nine—ten—ELEVEN!

I understood at last. That drugged sleep had lasted an hour and a half, and before I came to myself my watch had been deliberately set back to the minute at which I lost consciousness, in order to prevent me from suspecting that I had been searched, or that there was anything wrong about the affair.

Had I taken time for reflection I should probably have made up my mind to lose the Moscow express. In order to lull the suspicions of the conspirators, by making them believe I was their dupe, I should have let myself be taken to the hotel and put to bed in accordance with the kind instructions of my late host. In that case, no doubt, my watch would have been secretly put right again while I was asleep.

But I could not bear the idea of all my carefully planned arrangements being upset. Above all things, I desired to keep up my prestige with the superintendent of police, Rostoy, who regarded me as an invincible being possessed of almost magical powers. At the moment when the clock was striking I ought to have been walking into his room in the bureau of the Third Section.

Grinding my teeth with vexation, I very gently opened the door of the carriage, which was traveling noiselessly over the snow, and slipped out.

I had taken care to ascertain that no onlooker was near. As soon as the sleigh was 'round the corner of the street I hailed a public conveyance and directed the driver to take me to the police office.

I was only five minutes late in keeping my appointment. Detecting a look of slight surprise on the face of the superintendent, I apologized for keeping him waiting.

"It is my habit to be punctual, even in trifling matters like this," I remarked carelessly. "But the fact is I have been drugged and kidnapped since I saw you, and it took me five minutes to dispose of the rascals."

Rostoy stared at me with stupid incredulity.

"You are joking, Monsieur V——, I suppose," he muttered. "But, however, since you have arrived, there is your disguise. You will find everything in the pockets complete, including a handkerchief marked with the initials of the name you have chosen."

"Monsieur Rostoy, you are an able man, with whom it is pleasure to do business," I responded heartily.

The Russian swelled with pride at this compliment. I hastily changed clothes, shifting nothing from my discarded costume except a cigarette case which I had filled with the hotel cigarettes. My inquiry as to the Gregorides brand smoked by M. Petrovitch had not yet been answered.

"Surely you are not going to wear that linen shirt of yours right across Siberia!" exclaimed Rostoy, who never took his eyes off me.

I shrugged my shoulders.

"It is a whim of mine always to wear linen," I responded. "I am not a rheumatic subject. And, besides, I have no time to lose."

The superintendent threw a regretful look at the flannel shirt he had provided for me.

As soon as I had finished my preparations I handed a thick bundle of ruble notes to the superintendent.

"As much more when I come back safe," was all I said.

Rostoy snatched at his pay, his eyes sparkling with greed.

"Good-by and a good journey!" he cried as I strode out.

Once in the street, I had no difficulty in finding a sleigh, this time an open one, to convey me to the railway station. I glanced at my watch, which I had set by the church clock, and calculated that I should have a few minutes to spare.

But I had not allowed for Russian ideas as to time. As the sleigh drew up at the great terminus, and I came in view of the station clock, I saw that it was on the stroke of midnight.

Flinging the driver his fare I rushed toward the barrier.

"Moscow!" I shouted to the railway official in charge.

"The train has just left," was the crushing reply.

Chapter 7 The Race for Siberia

The unnatural strain I had put on my strength, undermined as it had been by the drugged vodka, gave way under this depressing failure, and for an instant I seriously thought of abandoning my effort to catch the Czar's messenger.

I could leave Colonel Menken to pursue his journey, taking care of himself as best he could, while I followed by a later train. But I had little thought of that, as to adopt such a course would be to abandon the gallant officer to his fate. Whatever the War Syndicate might or might not know or suspect about myself, there could be no doubt that they knew all there was to know about Menken, and that the Colonel would never be allowed to reach Dalny with his despatch, alive.

"Show me the passenger list," I demanded sternly, determined to use to the full the advantages conferred on me by my uniform.

The station inspector hastened to obey. He took me into the booking office, opened a volume, and there I read the name and destination of every passenger who had left for Moscow that night. It is by such precautions that the Russian police are enabled to control the Russian nation as the warders control the convicts in an English prison.

At the very head of the list I read the name of Colonel Menken, passenger to Dalny, on his imperial majesty's service.

It was incredible folly thus publicly to proclaim himself as an object of suspicion to the powerful clique engaged in thwarting the policy of their nominal ruler.

I glanced my eye down the list in search of some name likely to be that of an emissary of the Syndicate. It was with something like a shock that I came upon the conspicuous entry —

"The Princess Y— —, lady-in-waiting to H. I. M. the Dowager Empress, passenger to Port Arthur, on a visit to her uncle, commanding one of the forts."

Stamping my foot angrily, in order to impress the railway official, I said—

"Order a pilot engine immediately to take me to Moscow. Tell the driver he is to overtake the express, and enter the Moscow station behind it."

There was some demur, of course, and some delay. But I wore the livery of the dreaded Third Section, and my words were more powerful than if I had been the young man who wears the Russian crown.

By dint of curses, threats, blows and an occasional ruble note, I got my way. Indeed, I managed things so well that the railway officials did not even ask me for my name. I showed them my official badge; but when they made their report in the morning they would only be able to say that an inspector of the Secret Police had ordered a pilot engine to take him to Moscow in pursuit of the midnight express.

The impression which I was careful to convey, without putting it into words, was that I was on the track of an absconding Nihilist.

Within half an hour of my arrival at the terminus a light but powerful locomotive drew up on the main line of rails, with everything in readiness for an immediate start.

I leaped into the driver's cab, where I found the driver himself and two stokers hard at work increasing the head of steam, and gave the order to go.

The driver touched the tap, the whistle rang out once, and the wheels began to revolve. Ten seconds later we were beyond the station lights and facing the four hundred miles of frozen plain that lay between us and Moscow.

Every one has heard the story of this famous piece of road. The engineers of the line, accustomed to map out their routes in other countries with reference to the natural obstacles and the convenience of commerce, waited upon the great autocrat, Nicholas I., a very different man from his descendant, and asked him for instructions as to laying out the first railway in the Russian Empire.

The Czar called for a map of his dominions, and then, taking a ruler in his hand, drew a straight line between the old and new capitals.

And so the line has been made, a symbol to all who travel on it of the irresponsible might of the Russian Czardom.

It was not till we were fairly on our way, and the speed had risen to something like fifty miles an hour, that I realized what I had done in entering on this furious race.

I had never traveled on a detached engine before, and the sensation at first was quite unnerving.

Unlike a motor car, in which the hand of the driver has to be perpetually on the steering-gear, and his eye perpetually on the alert, the pilot engine seemed to be flung forward like a missile, guided by its own velocity, and clinging to the endless rails with its wheels as with iron claws. With the rush as of wind, with the roar as of a cataract, with the rocking as of an earthquake, the throbbing thing of iron sprang and fled through the night.

Hour after hour we rushed across the blinding desert of

snow, in which nothing showed except the flying disk of light cast by the engine lamps, and the red and white balls of fire that seemed to start, alight, and go out again as we frantically dashed past some wayside station.

As the speed increased the light pilot engine, not steadied by a long train of coaches, almost rose from the rails as it raced along. Over and over again I thanked my stars that there were no curves to be taken, and I blessed the memory of that famous ruler wielded by the hand of Nicholas I. Here and there, at some slight rise in the ground, the engine literally did leave the rails and skim through the air for a few yards, alighting with a jar that brought my teeth together like castanets, and rushing forward again.

I clung to a small brass hand-rail, and strained my eyes through the darkness. I could not have sat down, even had there been a seat provided for me—the pace was too tremendous. I was tired and unwell, and a slight feeling of headache and sickness began to gain on me, engendered by the vibration of the engine, the smell of oil, and the fearful heat of the furnace.

It was some hours since we had started, but it was still pitch dark, with the wintry blackness of a northern night. I leaned and gazed forward with dull eyes, when I was aware of two red sparks that did not grow and rush toward us as I expected.

Were we slackening speed by any chance? I turned to the engine driver, and pointed with my hand.

The grimy toiler nodded. Then making a trumpet of his hands he shouted above the rattle of the wheels—

"The rear-lights of the express!"

I drew out my watch and glanced at it by the light of the flaring stoke-hole. It was just half-past eight.

The time taken up on the journey between Petersburg and Moscow varies greatly according to the state of the weather and the amount of snow on the line. But even in the summer the best trains are allowed twelve hours, while the slow ones take nearly twenty-four. The special Siberian express was timed to reach the ancient capital of the czars at ten o'clock in the morning, and we had overtaken it with rather more than an hour to spare.

I ordered the driver to creep up gradually, but not to approach too near the hindmost coach of the train in front until Moscow was in sight.

Obedient to my instructions, he slackened speed by degrees, till we were rolling along at the same rate as the express, with a space of three or four hundred yards between us.

Presently a red flag was thrust out from a side window at the rear of the last coach and waved furiously. The driver of my engine responded with first a green and then a white signal, indication that there was no danger though caution was desirable.

The express perceptibly quickened its speed, but of course without our allowing it to get farther ahead. At last the spires of the Kremlin, and the green copper domes gleamed out across the waste, and I nodded to the driver to close up.

He managed the maneuver with the skill of an artist. Inch by inch we neared the guard's van in front, and our buffers were actually touching as the engine in front blew off steam and we slowed alongside the Moscow station.

Before the wheels of the express had ceased to move I was out on the platform, and running up to the guard of the express.

"I have come on the pilot engine from Petersburg," I told him hurriedly. "Tell no one of my arrival. Do not report the chase. If you are questioned, say that you have orders to say nothing. And now tell me which is the train for Dalny and Port Arthur, and when does it leave?"

The guard, thoroughly cowed, promised implicit obedience. He showed me a long corridor train with handsome sleeping cars and dining saloons, which was drawn up ready at another platform.

"That is the train which goes to Baikal," he told me. "If the ice on the lake will bear, rails may be laid right across it; if not, there will be sleighs to transport the passengers to a train on the other side. The train leaves at noon."

I thanked him and strolled off down the platform, glancing into the carriages of the newly-arrived train as I passed in search of the Czar's messenger.

I did not anticipate that any harm could have happened to him so soon after leaving Petersburg. The object of the conspirators would be defeated if Nicholas II. learned of any accident to his messenger in time to send another despatch. It was more likely, at least so I argued, that the Princess Y——would accompany her victim across Siberia, gradually worming her way into his confidence, and that only at the last moment would she show her hand.

It was with a slight start that I encountered the face of the fair emissary of M. Petrovitch, as she came to the door of her sleeping compartment and looked out.

I was delighted to observe that this time she did not

suspect me. In fact, she evidently mistook me for one of the ordinary station officials, for she gave me a haughty command:

"Go and see if there is a telegram for the Princess Y— —."

Making a respectful salute I hastened off in the direction of the telegraph office. On the way I interrupted a man in uniform carrying an envelope in his hand.

"For the Princess Y— —?" I demanded.

The man scowled at me and made as if to conceal the telegram. I saw that it was a case for a tip and handed him a ruble note, on which he promptly parted with his trust.

I turned around, and as soon as the messenger had moved off, I tore open the envelope and read the message. Fortunately, it was not in cipher, the rules against any such use of the wires, except by the Government, being too strict.

This is what I read:

"Our friend, who is now an inspector, will join you at Moscow. Look out for him. He has left his luggage with us, but does not know it."

Accident, which had hitherto opposed my designs, was favoring them at last. It was clear that Rostoy had betrayed me, and that Petrovitch had sent this wire to the Princess to put her on her guard. But what was the "luggage" which I was described as having left in the hands of M. Petrovitch?

I thought I knew.

Crumpling up the tell-tale message in my pocket, I darted into the telegraph office, and beckoned to the clerk in charge.

"On his majesty's secret service," I breathed in his ear, drawing him on one side. I showed him my police badge, and added, "An envelope and telegram form, quick!"

Overwhelmed by my imperative manner, he handed me

the required articles. I hastily scribbled:

"Our friend has parted with his luggage, though he does not know it. He has been unwell, but may follow you next week. To save trouble do not wire to us till you return."

Slipping this into the envelope, I addressed it to the Princess, and hastened back to the carriage where I had left her.

I found her fuming with impatience and scolding her maid, who looked on half awake. I handed her the bogus telegram with a cringing gesture. She snatched at it, tore off the cover and read, while I watched her furtively from under my lowered eyelashes.

The first part of the message evidently gave her the greatest pleasure. The second part, it was equally evident, puzzled and annoyed her.

"Fool! What is he afraid of now?" she muttered beneath her breath.

She stood gnawing her rose-red lips for a moment—even a night passed in the train could not make her look less charming—and then turned to me.

"That will do. No answer. Here, Marie, give this man a couple of rubles."

I received the gratuity with a look of satisfaction which must have surprised the tired waiting maid. In reality I had scored a most important point. Thanks to my suppression of the first message and my addition to the second, I had completely cut off communication between the agent of the Syndicate and its head in Petersburg, for a time; while I had lulled the beautiful plotter into a false security, by which I was likely to benefit.

My anxieties considerably lightened for the time being, I now renewed my search for Colonel Menken.

The train from Petersburg had emptied by this time, so I moved across the station to where the luxurious Manchurian express was being boarded by its passengers.

I got in at one end, and made my way slowly along the corridors, stepping over innumerable bags and other light articles. In a corner of the smoking car I came at last upon the man I sought.

Colonel Menken was a young man for his rank, not over thirty, with a fine, soldierly figure, handsome face and rather dandified air. He wore a brilliant uniform, which looked like that of some crack regiment of Guards. A cigar was in his mouth, and he was making a little nest for himself with rugs and books and papers, and a box of choice Havanas. A superb despatch box, with silver mounts, was plainly marked with his initials, also in silver.

I did not dare to choose a seat for myself in the same part of the train as the man whom I was anxious to guard. The oppressive powers wielded by the police of Russia are tolerated only on one condition, namely, that they are never abused to the disparagement of the social importance of the aristocracy.

Bearing this in mind, I proceeded to the coach set aside for the servants of the rich passengers, and contrived to secure a place close to that occupied in the day-time by the maid of the Princess.

Having more than an hour to spare, I now laid in a large stock of Turkish tobacco and cigarette papers, so as to have some means of beguiling the time on the long, wearisome run across Asia. I also bought a second-hand valise, and stocked it modestly with clothes. Finally I made a hearty breakfast in the station restaurant, and boarded the train a few minutes before it rolled out of Moscow.

Needless to say, I had introduced myself to the superintendent of the train, an official of great dignity and importance. As a police agent, of course I traveled free on the Government lines. The superintendent was good enough to offer me a spare bed in his private cabin at the end of the train, and during the run we became the best of friends.

But I must be excused from dwelling on the details of the journey, not the first I had taken on the great transasiatic line. My whole energies were absorbed in two tasks. In the first place, I had to gain the confidence of the maid, Marie, and in the second to prevent her mistress gaining the confidence of the messenger of the Czar.

"I hope that message I brought to the Princess did not contain any bad news?" I said to Marie as soon as I got a chance of addressing her.

This was when we were fairly on the way.

After first attending to her mistress, and seeing that she was comfortably settled, the maid was at liberty to look after herself, and I had seized the opportunity to render her a few trifling services with her luggage.

"I don't know, I'm sure," was the answer to my question. "The Princess tells me nothing of her secrets."

"Perhaps the Princess Y — — "

"Oh, let's call her Sophy," the maid interrupted crossly.

Needless to say I welcomed these symptoms that Marie was no great friend of her employer.

"Perhaps she has no secrets," I continued. "Have you been with her long?"

"Only six months," was the answer. "And I don't think I

shall stay much longer. But you're quite mistaken if you think Sophy is one of the innocent ones. She's always up to some mischief or other, though what it is, I don't know."

"If you stay with her a little longer, you may find out. And then, if it is anything political, you may make a good deal of money out of her."

The girl's eyes brightened.

"Keep your eyes open," I said. "Look out for any scraps of paper you see lying about. Keep a diary of the places Sophy goes to, and the people she sees. And when you have anything to tell, let me know. I will give you my address in Petersburg. And you may trust me to see that you come off well."

Marie readily agreed to all I asked of her. The understanding thus arrived at was destined to be of the greatest assistance to me. Indeed, it is not too much to say that to this young Russian girl it is due that the two greatest Powers in the Old World are not at this moment battling on the Afghan frontier.

We had hardly been an hour under way before I saw the two objects of my watchfulness seated side by side in the drawing-room car, apparently on the friendliest terms.

Dismayed by this rapid progress, as it seemed, on the part of the Princess, I reproached myself for not having warned Colonel Menken before we started.

I resolved to put him on his guard at the earliest possible moment, and with that view I hung about the smoking-car, waiting till I saw him return to his corner.

This was not for some hours. Fortunately, owing to the universal expectation of war, there were not many passengers proceeding to the Far East. The train was practically empty, and so when Colonel Menken had seated himself once more in the snug corner he had prepared for himself, I was able to approach him without fear of being overheard.

He was just lighting a cigar as I came up, and took no notice of my respectful salute till he had inhaled the tobacco smoke two or three times and expelled it through his nostrils to test the flavor.

At last he turned to me.

"Well?" he said with some sharpness. "What is the matter?"

"I have seen in the passenger list that you are traveling on the service of the Czar," I answered, "and I venture to place myself at your orders."

Colonel Menken scowled at me haughtily.

"Does that mean that you want a tip?" he sneered. "Or has some fool ordered you to shadow me?"

"Neither, Colonel," I replied. "I am a servant of the Czar, like yourself, as you may see from my uniform, and as I have reason to fear that there is an enemy of his majesty on the train, I wish to put you on your guard."

Menken gave a self-confident smile.

"I am pretty well able to take care of myself, I believe," he said boastfully. "As for the Nihilists, I no longer believe in their existence. You may point out the man you suspect, if you like, of course."

"It is not a man, Colonel, it is a woman."

"In that case the adventure promises to be interesting. I do not know any of the women on board except the Princess Y ——."

"You know her!" I allowed a note of surprise to appear in

my voice.

"The Princess is related to me," the Czar's messenger declared, with a rebuking frown. "I presume she is not the object of your suspicions?"

"And if she were?"

"If she were, I should tell you that you had made a very absurd mistake, my good fellow. The Princess is in the confidence of the Dowager Empress; she is perfectly aware of the object of my mission, and she has just promised me that if I carry it out successfully she will become my wife."

Chapter 9 The Betrothal of Delilah

Colonel Menken regarded me with ironical contempt as I tried to apologize for my hinted distrust of his betrothed.

"That will do, my man. I shall tell the Princess of your blunder, and I can assure you she will be heartily amused by it."

"At least you will remember that I wear his imperial majesty's uniform," I ventured. "And, however much I have been misled as to the intentions of her highness, I submit that I am entitled to secrecy on your part."

"Am I to understand that some one has given you orders referring to the Princess? I thought this was simply some idle suspicion of your own?"

"My instructions were to watch over your safety, without letting you perceive it, and to take particular note of any one who seemed to be trying to form your acquaintance on the journey. If you now denounce me to her highness, she will be annoyed, and in any case I shall be of no further use to you."

"So much the better," the Colonel said rudely. "I consider your being here at all as an act of impertinence. If I engage to say nothing to the Princess—who, as you say, might be annoyed—will you undertake to leave me alone for the future?"

"I will undertake to leave the train at Tomsk," I replied.

Colonel Menken closed with this offer, which was meant as a delusive one. I had selected the first important stopping-place at which the train waited sufficiently long for me to procure the materials of a fresh disguise.

I took the train superintendent into my confidence, as far as to say that I wished to assume a false character for the remainder of the journey in order to be better able to play the spy on the object of my suspicion. We agreed that one of the train attendants should be put off at Tomsk, and that I should take his place.

After my scene with the Colonel, I could not venture to do much in the way of overlooking them. But I made the best use of my friendship with Marie, and she reported to me regularly what she observed of the doings of her mistress.

"It is my belief that Sophy is going to marry that stupid Colonel," she informed me, not long after I had heard of the engagement. "Why? I can't think. He has no brains, not much money, and I am certain she is not in love with him."

"There has been a quarrel of some kind between those two," she reported later on. "Colonel Menken has been questioning Sophy about her reason for going to Port Arthur just now, when it may be attacked by the Japanese."

All this time the Princess had made no move to possess herself of the despatch which Menken was carrying—the real object of her presence on board the train.

When Tomsk was reached, I went off into the town and procured different hair and beard so as to effect a complete change in my appearance. The disguise was clumsy enough, but, after all, neither the Colonel nor his companion had had many opportunities of studying my personal appearance.

In the little cabin of my friend the superintendent I carried out the transformation, and finished by donning the livery of the railway restaurant service.

Thus equipped, I proceeded to lay the table at which the betrothed pair usually took their meals together.

As soon as the next meal, which happened to be dinner, was ready, I proceeded to wait upon them. They noticed the change of waiters, and asked me what had become of my predecessor.

"He got off at Tomsk," I told them. This was true—the getting rid of the waiter whose place I wished to take had been a simple matter. It must be remembered that I found myself everywhere received as an inspector attached to the secret police, the dreaded Third Section, and, in consequence, my word was law to those I had to deal with.

I added with an assumed air of mysterious consequence, "The Inspector of Police also left the train at Tomsk. It is asserted that he is going to make an important arrest."

Colonel Menken laughed. Then turning to the beautiful woman who sat facing him across the small table, he said smilingly,

"It is lucky the inspector did not arrest you, my dear."

"Why, what do you mean?" she demanded.

"Simply that this officer, according to his own account, was charged to watch over and protect your devoted servant, and in the exercise of his functions he was good enough to hint to me that you were a suspicious character, of whom I should do well to be on my guard."

"Infamous! The wretch! Why didn't you tell me this before?"

"I promised the fellow not to. He was afraid of getting into trouble, and as he had only blundered out of zeal, I let him off."

"And he has left the train. Why, I wonder?"

"I ordered him to."

The Princess Y—— looked less and less pleased. A minute later, I caught her stealthily glancing in my direction, and realized that her keen wits were already at work, connecting my appearance on the scene with the disappearance of the inspector.

The next day, Colonel Menken and his betrothed took their seats at a different table in the restaurant of the train.

I saw the meaning of this maneuver. It was of course a test by which the Princess Y— — sought to learn if I was a spy, appointed to replace the inspector. I took care not to assist her by following them to the new table; on the contrary, I refused the offer of my brother waiter, who was honest enough not to wish to take my tips from me.

When we reached Irkutsk, I had another proof that the Princess was beginning to feel uneasy. Marie informed me that her mistress had ordered her to go into the town and send off a telegram, as she would not trust the railway officials.

The message, which my ally faithfully reported to me, was addressed to Petrovitch himself and ran as follows:

Received wire from you at Moscow reporting our friend ill, and telling me not to wire you again till my return. I now fear some mistake. All going well otherwise.

We were carried across the frozen Baikal amid a furious snowstorm. Huddled up in thick furs, and fighting to keep our blood circulating under the leaden pressure of the cruel frost, there was no time to think of conspiracies.

But on resuming the journey on the other side of the lake, I saw that the cunning agent of the War Party was maturing some decisive attempt on the messenger of peace. The talks of the lovers became closer and more confidential, the manner of Colonel Menken grew daily more devoted and absorbed, and Marie described her mistress as laboring under an extraordinary excitement.

At last, on the very day the train crossed the Chinese frontier on the way to Mukden, Marie came to me with a decisive report.

"Sophy has won!" she declared. "I overheard them talking again last night. Ever since they left Tomsk they have been having a dispute, Sophy declaring that the Colonel did not love her, because he suspected her, and he, the stupid creature, swearing that he trusted her entirely. It appears she had got out of him that he was carrying a paper of some kind, and so she said that unless he gave her this paper to keep till they reached Dalny or Port Arthur, she would not believe in him, nor have anything more to say to him.

"In the end, she was too many for him. Last night he gave her the paper in a sealed envelope, and I saw her take it from her breast before she undressed last night."

"Where is it? What has she done with it?" I demanded anxiously.

"I can't tell you that. She had it in her hand when she dismissed me for the night. It looked to me as though she meant to break the seal and read it."

Full of the gravest forebodings, I hurried to the rear of the train, got out my inspector's uniform, though without effecting any change in my facial appearance, and made my way to the smoking-car.

Colonel Menken, who had just finished breakfast, was settling himself down to a cigar and an illustrated magazine.

He gazed up at me in astonishment, as he perceived the change in my costume.

"So the Princess was right!" he exclaimed angrily. "You are another policeman."

I bowed.

"And charged, like the last, to protect me from my cousin and future wife!"

"From the person who has robbed you of the Czar's autograph letter to the Emperor of Japan, yes!"

Menken recoiled, thunderstruck.

"You knew what I was carrying?"

"As well as I know the contents of the telegram which the Princess sent from Irkutsk to the head of the Manchurian Syndicate—the man who has sworn that the Czar's letter shall never be delivered."

Colonel Menken staggered to his feet, bewildered, angry, half induced to threaten, and half to yield.

"You must be lying! Sophy never left my sight while we were at Irkutsk!"

"We can discuss that later. Will you, or will you not, reclaim his majesty's letter—the letter entrusted to your honor?"

Menken turned white.

"I—I will approach the Princess," he stammered, obviously divided between fear of losing her, and dread of myself and any action I might take.

"That will not do for me," I said sternly. "I can only make you this offer: Come with me at once to this lady's sleeping berth and regain the despatch, and I will agree to say no more about it; refuse, and I shall report the whole affair to his majesty personally."

"Who are you?" inquired the dismayed man.

"That is of no consequence. You see my uniform—let that be enough for you."

He staggered down the car. I followed, and we reached

the car where the Princess was at the moment engaged, with Marie's aid, in putting the last touches to her toilet.

She looked up at our appearance, gave an interrogative glance first at Menken and then, at me, and evidently made up her mind.

"What is it, gentlemen?"

"The—the paper I gave—that you offered to—that—in short, I want it immediately," faltered my companion.

"I have no paper of yours, and I do not know what you are talking about, my friend," said the Princess Y—— with the calmest air in the world.

Menken uttered a cry of despair.

"The letter, the letter I gave you last night—it was a letter from the Czar," he exclaimed feebly.

"I think you must have dreamed it," said the Princess with extreme composure. "Marie, have you seen any letter about?"

"No, your highness," returned the servant submissively.

"If you think there is anything here, you are welcome to look," her mistress added with a pleasant smile. "As for me, I never keep letters, my own or anybody else's. *I always tear them up.*"

And with these words, and another smile and a nod, she stepped gracefully past us, and went to take her seat in the part of the train reserved for ladies.

Somewhere, doubtless, on the white Manchurian plain we had crossed in the night, the fragments of the imperial peacemaker's letter were being scattered by the wind.

Menken's face had changed utterly in the last minute. He resembled an elderly man.

"Tell the Czar that I alone am to blame," were his last words.

Before I could prevent him, he had drawn a revolver from his pocket, and put two bullets through his head.

Chapter 10 *The Answer of the Mikado*

A week later, that is to say, on the 8th of February, 1904, I was in Tokio.

The behavior of the Princess Y— — on hearing of the death of her victim had been a strange mixture of heartlessness and hysterical remorse.

At the first sound of the fatal shots, she came rushing to the scene of the tragedy, and cast herself on the floor of the corridor beside the dead man, seizing his hands, crying his name aloud, and weeping frantically.

When I tried to raise her, so that the body might be removed, she turned on me fiercely.

"This is your fault!" she cried. "Who are you, and how dared you interfere with me?"

"As you see by my uniform, I am an inspector of police attached to the Third Section."

She gazed at me searchingly for a moment, and then, lowering her voice, and bringing her lips to my ear, she said with intense energy:

"It is a lie. I am here by the orders of the Minister himself, as you must know well. You are acting against us, whoever you are."

"I am acting by order of the Czar," I responded.

She smiled scornfully.

"I expect that is another lie. You could not have got so far as you have unless you had some one else behind you. Poor Nicholas!—Every one knows what he is, and that he has less power than any other man in Russia. Are you Witte's man, I wonder?"

"You are a bold woman to question me," I said. "How do you know that I am not going to arrest you for stealing and destroying the Czar's letter?"

"I should not remain long under arrest," was the significant answer. She gave me another searching look, and muttered to herself, "If I did not know that he was safe in the hands of my friends in Petersburg I should think you must be a certain Monsieur — —"

She broke off without pronouncing my name, and turned away.

At Mukden, the next stopping place, the Princess Y— — left the train, no doubt intending to travel back to Russia and report her success.

In the meantime, I had reason to think she had notified her friends in Manchuria to keep an eye on me.

All the way to Dalny I felt by that instinct which becomes second nature to a man of my profession that I was under surveillance. I detected a change in the manner of my friend the train superintendent. My trifling luggage was carefully searched. In the night when I was asleep some one went through my pockets. I was able to see that even the contents of my cigarette case, which I had not opened since leaving Petersburg, had been turned out and put back again.

As the train neared Dalny I began to feel a little nervous. I had a dread of being stopped on my way to embark on board the steampacket which was still running to Tokio.

The train drew up at last, at the end of its five-thousand-mile-run, and I stepped off it to the platform, carrying my valise in my hand.

The platform was literally swarming with spies, as it was

easy for a man of my experience to detect. I walked calmly through them to the cab-stand, and hailed a droshky.

The driver, before starting off, exchanged a signal almost openly with a stout man in plain clothes, who dogged me from the railway carriage.

Presently I sighted the steamer, alongside the principal wharf, with the smoke pouring out of its funnel, all ready to start.

The cabman whipped his horse and drove straight past the steamer.

"Where are you going?" I shouted.

"To the Custom House first; it is the regulation," was the answer.

Taking out my long neglected case, I placed a cigarette between my lips, and asked the driver for some matches.

He passed me a wooden box. I struck several, but each went out in the high wind before igniting the tobacco.

I was making another attempt as the droshky drew up outside the steps of the Custom House. I dismounted negligently, while one of the officials came and clutched my luggage. Then I walked slowly up the steps, pausing in the porch to strike a fresh match.

A porter snatched the box from my hand. "Smoking is forbidden," he said roughly. "Wait till you are out again."

I shrugged my shoulders, pinched the burning end of the cigarette, which I retained in my mouth, and sauntered with an air of supreme indifference after the man who was carrying my bag.

He led me into a room in which a severe-looking official was seated at a desk.

"Your papers," he demanded.

I produced the papers with which I had been furnished by Rostoy.

The customs official scrutinized them, evidently in the hope of discovering some flaw.

"On what business are you going to Tokio?" he demanded.

I smiled.

"Since when have the police of the Third Section been obliged to render an account of themselves to the officers of the customs?" I asked defiantly.

"How do I know that you are not a Japanese spy?"

I laughed heartily.

"You must be mad. How do I know that you are not a Nihilist?" I retorted.

The customs officer turned pale. I saw that my chance shot had gone home. The Russian imperial services are honeycombed by revolutionary intrigues.

"Well, I shall detain your luggage for examination," he declared.

This time I pretended the greatest agitation. Of course, the more I resisted the more he insisted. In the end he allowed me to depart without my person being searched. The fact is I had convinced him that he held an important prize in my worthless valise.

I was just in time to catch the steamer. As I crossed the gangway, a man dressed like a coal-trimmer turned on me a last careful scrutiny, and remarked,

"Your cigarette has gone out, Mister."

"Can you give me a light? Thank you!" I struck a match,

drew a puff of smoke, and handed him back the box. Then I walked on board, the gangway was drawn in, and the Japanese steamer headed out to the open sea.

On reaching Tokio I experienced some difficulty in obtaining an audience of the Japanese ruler.

I was obliged to announce my name. It will hardly be believed, but the chamberlain whom I had entrusted with the important secret, brought back the answer that the Mikado had never heard of me!

"Tell his imperial majesty that there is no monarch of Europe, and only two of Asia, who could say the same. I am here as the confidential plenipotentiary of the Czar, with an autograph letter addressed to the Mikado, and I respectfully ask leave to present it in person."

Such a demand of course could not be refused. But even now the haughty Japanese did not receive me in the privacy of his own cabinet. On the contrary, I found myself introduced into the State Council-Room, in which his majesty was seated at a table surrounded by his chief advisers.

In particular I remarked the venerable Yamagata, conqueror of China, and the round bullet-head of Oyama, the future overthrower of Kuropatkin.

On the table was spread out a large map, or rather plan, of the entire theater of war, including Manchuria, Korea, Japan and the seas between. A man in naval uniform was standing beside the imperial chair, with an expectant look on his face.

All eyes were turned upon me at my entrance. The Mikado beckoned to me to approach him.

"Is it true that you bring me a letter from the Russian Emperor?" he asked abruptly. "We have received information that such a letter was on its way, but that the bearer was murdered on the Manchurian railway four days ago."

"Your majesty's information is substantially correct," I answered. "The messenger, a Colonel Menken, was seduced into parting with his despatch, and committed suicide in consequence."

"Well, and what about yourself?"

"Foreseeing that the unscrupulous men who have been trying to force on a war between his Russian majesty and your majesty would leave no stone unturned to intercept this despatch, the Czar wrote a duplicate with his own hand, which he entrusted to me, in the hope that I might baffle the conspirators."

"Where is it?"

"I endeavored to conceal it by unstitching the front of the shirt I am wearing, and sewing it up between the folds.

"Unfortunately I was drugged at a dinner party in Petersburg just before starting. I was unconscious for an hour and a half, and I fear that the opponents of peace have taken advantage of the opportunity to find and rob me of the letter. But I will see, with your majesty's permission."

The Mikado made no answer. Amid a breathless silence, with all the room watching my movements, I tore open my shirt-front and extracted a paper.

It was blank.

"So," commented the Japanese Emperor, sternly, "you have no such credentials as you boasted of having."

"Pardon me, sire. Anticipating that the War Party would suspect the object of my mission, and would resort to some such step to defeat it, I purposely provided them with a document to steal, believing that when they had robbed me of it they would allow me to proceed unmolested. My real credentials are here."

I drew out my cigarette case, found the partially smoked cigarette I had had in my mouth when I ran the gauntlet of the spies at Dalny, and proceeded to cut off the paper. On the inner surface these words were written in the hand of the Czar:

The bearer of this, M. V— —, has my full confidence, and is authorized to settle conditions of peace.

Nicholas.

As I respectfully placed the scrap of paper, with its charred edges, in the Mikado's hand, I was conscious of a profound sensation in the room. Aged statesmen and brilliant commanders bent eagerly across the table to learn the character of the message thus strangely brought to its destination.

His majesty read the brief note aloud. It was received with a murmur, not entirely of satisfaction I was surprised to note.

Seeing that the Mikado made no remark, I ventured to say:

"I hope that the extreme character of the measures adopted by the Czar to assure your majesty of his peaceful sentiments will have the effect of convincing you that they are genuine."

The Emperor of Japan glanced around his council board as if to satisfy himself that he and his advisers were of one mind before replying:

"I appreciate the zeal and the extraordinary skill with which you have carried out your mission. I regret that I cannot give you a favorable answer to take back to your nation."

I was thunderstruck at this exordium. Slightly raising his

voice, the Mikado went on:

"Tell the Emperor of Russia that I do not distrust his sincerity, but I distrust his power. The monarch who cannot send a letter through his dominions in safety; who has to resort to stratagems and precautions like these to overcome the opposition of his own subjects, is not the ruler of his empire.

"Why, sir, do you suppose that if I had a message to send to my brother in St. Petersburg I should have to stoop to arts like these? That any subject of mine would dare to plot against me, to seduce my messengers, to drug and rob them? Incredible! The tale you have told me completely confirms everything I and my advisers have already heard with regard to the Russian Government. It is a ship without a captain, on which the helm is fought for and seized by different hands in turn. To-day the real rulers of Russia are the men who are bent on war—and who, while we are talking, have actually begun the war!"

I gazed around the Council-Room, unable to believe my ears.

"Yes," the stern sovereign continued, "while you, sir, were entering the Inland Sea, charged with this offer of peace"—his majesty tossed the precious piece of paper on the table with a look of disdain—"a Russian gunboat, the *Korietz*, was firing the first shot of the war at one of my squadrons off Chemulpo."

The glances directed by those present at the naval officer behind the imperial chair convinced me that he had just brought the fatal news to the Council.

"And now," added the Mikado, "I will give my reply to the real masters of Russia—to the directors of the *Korietz*."

He nodded to the naval officer, who walked across the floor to a box on the wall like a telephone receiver, and pressed a button.

"That," his majesty explained, "is the signal for a flotilla of torpedo boats to enter the harbor of Port Arthur and blow up the Russian fleet."

I think a faint cry of remonstrance or misgiving must have escaped me. The Japanese monarch frowned, and his voice took a still sterner ring.

"Go back to your unfortunate master, and tell him that when he can send me a public envoy, in the light of day, to ask for peace, and to undertake the fulfilment of the pledges which his Ministers have broken, I will grant his request."

Chapter 11 Who Smoked the Gregorides Brand

I left the presence of the Japanese Emperor deeply disheartened.

It is true I had myself foretold this failure, and that his Japanese majesty and his advisers had been good enough to compliment me in almost extravagant terms on the energy and resourcefulness I had shown in baffling the enemies of peace.

But I am unaccustomed to defeat, no matter what are the odds against me, and I felt that the first point in the game had been scored against by the formidable woman whose beauty and strangely composite character had fascinated me, even while I was countermining her.

For my work was not yet over. Indeed, it had but just begun.

I had not succeeded in averting war between the two great Powers of Asia. But I hoped to thwart the efforts which I feared would be made to extend the conflagration to Europe.

As soon as I had found myself once more on civilized ground, I had despatched a cable to my Paris office, announcing my whereabouts and asking for information.

The reader may be excused if he has forgotten a little episode which marked my stay in Petersburg. I had noticed something peculiar and at the same time familiar in the scent of the tobacco smoked by Petrovitch, the financial adventurer whose scheme to enrich himself and a corrupt clique of courtiers out of the spoils of Korea and China was the true cause of the war.

By a ruse I had secured one of the cigarettes, smoked by this dangerous plotter, and having ascertained that it bore the mark *Gregorides, Crown Aa*, had instructed my staff to ascertain the history of this particular make of cigarettes.

While I was resting in my hotel in Tokio, waiting for the reply to my cable, I was honored by a visit from no less a personage than Privy Councillor Katahashi, President of the Imperial Bank of Japan.

"I have come," the Privy Councillor explained as soon as the door was closed, "to express the high sense of your ability and devotion which we all possess, and to ask if it is possible for Japan to secure your services."

Deeply gratified by this proposal, I was obliged to explain that I was already retained in the interest of Russia.

"But what interest?" Mr. Katahashi persisted. "It is clear that you are not acting on behalf of that group which has just succeeded in its purpose of forcing a war."

"That is so," I admitted. "It is no breach of confidence—in fact, I serve my employers by assuring you that my efforts are directed toward peace."

"In that case there can be no antagonism between us, surely. Is it not possible for you and me—I say nothing about our respective Governments—to co-operate for certain purposes?

"I know enough of the conditions which prevail in the Russian Court to feel pretty sure that it was not Nicholas II. who originally sought you out, and entrusted you with this mission," the Japanese statesman added.

"At the close of the last war in this part of the world," the Privy Councillor went on, "Japan was robbed of the fruit of her victories by an alliance of three Powers, Russia, Germany, and France. This time we know that England will support us against any such combination. Thanks to King Edward VII. we have nothing to fear. His diplomacy, moreover, has secured the powerful influence of France on the side of peace. Although nominally allied with the Czar, we know that the French Government is determined to limit the area of the war, and to take no part against us, except in one event."

"You mean," I put in, "in the event of an attack by England on Russia."

"Exactly. And therefore we know that King Edward is making it his particular care that no cause of conflict shall arise."

He paused, and glanced at me as though he considered that he had sufficiently indicated the source from which my instructions were received.

I contented myself with bowing.

"We know, also, that the most restless and ambitious of living monarchs has been bending his whole thoughts and schemes, ever since he ascended the throne, to one supreme end —the overthrow of the British Empire by a grand combination of all the other Powers of the world. If that monarch can force on a general strife in which England will be involved on the side of Japan, while practically every other European Power is leagued against her, M. Petrovitch and his timber concessions will have done their work."

I drew a deep breath as I looked at the Japanese statesman with a questioning gaze.

As if in answer to my unspoken query, a waiter of the hotel knocked at the door in the same moment, and brought me the long-expected cable from my agent in Europe.

I tore it open and read:

Cigarettes Gregorides Crown Aa special brand

manufactured to order of Marx, Berlin, tobacconist to German Emperor.

I looked up from reading the telegram to see the eyes of the Japanese Privy Councillor fixed upon me with the inscrutable, penetrating gaze of the Oriental.

"The message you have just received bears on the subject of our conversation, does it not?" he inquired, but in the tone of one who does not doubt what the answer will be.

With the caution which has become a habit with me, I read the cable through carefully for the second time, and then placed it on the fire, where it was instantly consumed.

The Japanese statesman smiled.

"You forget, I think, M. V— —, that you have come here as the emissary of a sovereign with whom we are at war, and that, consequently, we cannot afford to respect your privacy.

"I have a copy in my pocket," he went on urbanely. "You have felt some curiosity about a particular brand of cigarettes, and your friends have just informed you that they are those supplied to the German Emperor."

I looked at Mr. Katahashi with new respect.

"Your secret service is well managed, sir," I observed.

"Such a compliment from such a quarter is an ample reward for what little pains I may have taken."

"Then it is you who are— —?"

"The organizer of our secret service during the war?—I am."

"But you are a banker?" I turned my eyes to the card by which Mr. Katahashi had announced his visit.

The Japanese gave another of his subtle smiles—those peculiar smiles of the Oriental which make the keenest-witted man of the West feel that he is little better than a blunderer.

"I came here prepared to take you into my confidence," he said gravely. "I am well aware that it is the only safe course in dealing with the Bismarck of underground diplomacy.

"I am equally well aware," the Privy Councillor added, "that a secret confided to Monsieur V—— is as safe as if it had been told in confidence to a priest of Buddha, for whom the penalty of betrayal is to be flayed alive."

Chapter 12 *The Secret Service of Japan*

"Three years ago," Mr. Katahashi proceeded, "when we first recognized that Japan would be obliged to fight Russia for her existence as a free and independent country, his imperial majesty the Mikado appointed me head of the intelligence department.

"I perceived that it would be necessary for me to establish centers in the chief European capitals, and to have at my command a corps of agents whose comings and goings would not attract the attention that is usually given to the movements of persons connected with the staff of an embassy.

"In our case precautions were necessary which would not have been recognized in the case of another country.

"On the one hand, our Government has laid to heart the profound advice of Herbert Spencer, that whatever is done for Japan should be done by Japanese.

"On the other hand, our people have characteristic racial features which make it practically impossible for a Japanese to disguise himself as a Western European, so as to deceive European eyes.

"It was therefore necessary to provide an excuse for distributing Japanese agents over the West without the true reason of their presence being known.

"I solved this problem by founding the Imperial Bank of Japan."

"But, surely!" I exclaimed, "the Imperial Bank of Japan is a *bona fide* concern? Its shares are regularly quoted on the stock exchanges. It negotiates loans, and carries on the ordinary business of a bank?"

"Certainly. Why not? You forget that Japan is not a rich country. What we lack in gold, we are obliged to make up in ingenuity and devotion. Thanks to this idea of mine, the secret service of Japan pays for itself, and even earns a small profit."

It gave me something like a cold shock to comprehend the character of this people whom the Russians had so recklessly provoked to draw the sword.

I thought of the intelligence departments of some Western Powers, of the rank corruption that reigned on the Neva, where every secret had its price; of the insane conceit of Berlin, which had forgotten nothing and learned nothing since the days of Moltke; of the luxurious laziness of Pall Mall, where superannuated soldiers dozed in front of their dusty pigeon-holes after apoplectic lunches, and exercised their wits chiefly in framing evasive answers suited to the intelligence of the House of Commons.

And beside these pictures I placed this of the prosperous commercial house, founded by the man before me, a man whose salary would probably be sniffed at by a deputy-assistant controller in the British War Office.

A bank, paying its way, and adding to the revenues of Japan, and yet every member of its staff a tireless spy, ready to go anywhere and risk everything on behalf of his native country!

Mr. Katahashi seemed to ignore the effect produced on my mind by his modest explanation.

"I have told you this," he resumed, "because if I can succeed in satisfying you that we are both working for the same ends, or at least against the same enemy, I hope it will be agreeable to you to co-operate with me."

I drew my brows together in anxious thought. In spite of

the flattery and deference of the Privy Councillor I could not but feel that I should be the junior partner in any such combination as he proposed, or, rather, I should find myself an instrument in the hands of one whose methods were strange to me.

"Although his imperial majesty was not familiar with your name, you must not suppose that your reputation is not known in the right quarters. I have a very full report on your work in my office. I had intended from the first to engage your services if we required any Western aid; and, as a matter of fact, I was on the eve of sending you a retainer, when I heard I had been anticipated by — — "

"By Lord Bedale," I put in swiftly.

"By Lord Bedale, certainly," the Japanese acquiesced with a polite bow and smile.

"After your interview with him, I lost sight of you," my extraordinary companion went on. "Your wonderful transformation into a Little Englander of the Peace-at-any-Price school threw my agents off the scent. But I heard of your interview with Nicholas II."

"You did!"

Mr. Katahashi nodded.

"I recognized you in that transaction. I even guessed that you might make an attempt to carry through a message from the Czar. But, knowing the influences arrayed against you, I never expected you to succeed. Your appearance in our Council-Room was a triumph on which I congratulate you warmly.

"And now," the Mikado's Privy Councillor continued, "there remain two questions:

"Supposing you are satisfied that the real author of this war is not any one in Russia, but a certain monarch who smokes cigarettes made by the house of Gregorides—

"And that the same ambitious ruler is now weaving his snares to entangle Great Britain, in short your own employer, the — —"

"Marquis of Bedale," I again slipped in.

Again the same polite but incredulous bow and smile from the Japanese statesman.

"Would you be willing to accept a retainer from us?"

I sat upright, frowning.

The somewhat haughty attitude of the Emperor of Japan still rankled within me.

"I will accept a retainer from his majesty the Mikado," I announced stiffly. "From no one else."

Mr. Katahashi looked thoughtful.

"I will see what can be done," he murmured. "The second question— —"

There was a momentary hesitation in his manner.

"I have just spoken to you of the precept of the great English philosopher."

"It was, if I remember rightly, that you should employ only Japanese in the service of Japan?"

The Privy Councillor bowed.

"Therefore, you will see, we are obliged to make a proposal which may seem to you unusual—perhaps unreasonable."

"And this proposal is?" I asked, with undisguised curiosity.

"That you should become a Japanese."

I threw myself back in my chair, amazed.

"Your Excellency, I am an American citizen."

"So I have understood."

"An American citizen is on a level with royalty."

"That is admitted."

"Even the Dowager Empress of China, when engaging me in her service, though she raised my ancestors to the rank of marquises, did not ask me to forego my citizenship of the United States."

"That is not necessary," the Privy Councillor protested.

"Explain yourself, if you will be so good."

"A man may be an American citizen, although by birth he is a Frenchman, a German, or even a negro. You yourself are a Pole, I believe."

I could only bow.

"Now I do not propose that you should relinquish your political allegiance, but only that you should exchange your Polish nationality for a Japanese one."

"But how, sir?"

"It is very simple. By being adopted into a Japanese family."

I sat and stared at the Japanese statesman, with his mask-like face and impenetrable eyes. I seemed to be in some strange dream.

Who shall judge the ways of the Asiatic! This daring organizer, a match for the most astute minds of the West, believed that he could only make sure of fidelity by persuading me to go through what seemed the comedy of a mock adoption, a ceremony like the blood brotherhood of an African tribe.

"And suppose I consent, into what family do you purpose to introduce me?"

The Privy Councillor's look became positively

affectionate as he responded:

"If you would honor me by becoming my kinsman?"

I rose to my feet, shaking my head slowly.

"I appreciate the compliment your Excellency pays me. But, as we have just now agreed, an American citizen has no equals except royalty. Let us return to the German Emperor and his designs. If I cannot serve you directly I may be able to do so indirectly."

The Japanese made no attempt to press his proposal.

Instead he plunged into a discussion of the intrigues which radiated from Berlin.

"In nearly all the international difficulties and disagreements of the last twenty years," he said, "it is possible to trace the evil influence of Germany.

"To German sympathy, a secret encouragement, was due the wanton invasion of Cape Colony by the Boers. To the Kaiser, and his promises of support, was due the hopeless defiance of the United States by Spain. The same Power tried to drag Great Britain into collision with your Republic over the miserable concerns of Venezuela. For years, Germany has been secretly egging on the French to raise troubles against the English in Egypt. In the same spirit, the Sultan has been abetted, first against England and next against Russia.

"All these schemes have been spoiled by the action of King Edward VII. in establishing cordial relations with France, and even to a certain extent with Russia.

"Now Wilhelm II. has taken advantage of the attraction of France to England, to draw nearer to Russia. He has secured in his interest some of the most influential personages at the Russian Court. The Anglophobe grand dukes, the fire-eaters of the Admiralty, are all his sworn allies.

"But that is not the worst.

"By some means which I have not yet been able to trace, the Kaiser seems to have acquired a peculiar hold over Nicholas II.

"The whole policy of Russia seems to be tinged by this influence. Even where the instigation of Germany is not directly apparent, yet in a hundred ways it is clear that the Russian Government is playing the German game. The cause of all this is a riddle, a riddle which it is for you to solve."

"For me?"

The words escaped me involuntarily. I had listened with growing uneasiness to the Privy Councillor's revelations.

"Undoubtedly. You have facilities which no one else possesses. You enjoy the confidence of the Czar. You cannot be suspected of any selfish designs, still less of any hostile feeling against Wilhelm II., who is understood to be almost your personal friend."

"I never allow personal friendships to influence me in the discharge of my duty."

"It is because I believe that, that I am talking to you like this," Mr. Katahashi responded quickly.

"Well!" he added after a short silence, "what do you say?"

"I must have the night to decide."

The Japanese Privy Councillor rose to say good-by.

After he had gone I sat up late into the night considering how far I could serve my employer in England by entering into the projects of the secret service of Japan.

In the morning, I was still undecided, but on the whole it seemed to me that it would be better to act independently.

I was considering how to convey this decision to the Mikado's minister, when he again presented himself before me.

His manner was deeply agitated. It was evident that he came to make a communication of the highest importance.

Instead of taking the chair I offered him, he stood regarding me with an expression that seemed one of awe.

"Monsieur V——," he said at length, "your conditions are accepted by his imperial majesty."

"What conditions?" I asked, bewildered for the moment.

"Last night you informed me that an American citizen occupied the same rank as royalty."

"Well?"

"The Mikado offers to make you a member of the imperial family by adoption, and one of his majesty's cousins has consented to make you his son!"

Chapter 13 His Imperial Highness

In these days, when princes resign their rank to marry commoners, and queens elope with tutors, it is probable that most Western minds will see nothing out of the way in the condescension of the Japanese ruler in admitting a diplomatic agent to the honor of the imperial cousinship.

But the dynasty of Japan is the most illustrious in the world, excepting only that of Great Britain. Like Edward VII., the Mikado traces his lineage back to pagan gods. From the days of the famous Empress Jimmu, an unbroken line of sacred sovereigns has filled the throne of the Realm of the Rising Sun during more than two thousand years.

Mr. Katahashi was evidently pleased to see that I appreciated to the full the tremendous honor accorded to me.

"An imperial carriage is waiting to convey you to the Palace," he said. "But it will not be becoming for you to wear that uniform. I have brought you a Japanese dress."

An attendant came into the room bearing a gorgeous robe of green silk embroidered with golden chrysanthemums.

I put it on like one in a dream. The Privy Councillor with his own hands girt around my waist the two weapons, sacred from time immemorial to the use of the Japanese noble, the sword with which to behead his friend, and the dagger with which to disembowel himself.

Needless to say, I had no expectation that I should ever have occasion to regard these magnificently embellished weapons in any other light than as ornamental badges of rank.

As we rode to the Palace, I could not forbear contrasting this splendid treatment with that which I had been accustomed to receive from some of the European sovereigns to whom I had rendered important services.

Even the German Kaiser, who trusted me more than the head of his own police, who talked to me almost on the footing of an intimate friend, had never offered me so much as the coveted "von" before my name—had not given me even the pretty Red Eagle which is lavished on second-rate generals and lords-in-waiting.

I became well-nigh appalled as I contrasted the sluggish conversation, the hide-bound officialism, the stereotyped and sleepy methods of the Western Powers with the sleepless energy, the daring initiative, the desperate industry and courage of this rejuvenated Eastern race.

What could any of these obsolete European Governments effect against a nation which was really a vast secret society of forty-five millions, directed by a sacred chief, and wielding all the mechanical resources of the West with the almost inhuman subtlety and ruthlessness of the Orient?

"Anything can be done for money." This maxim, which is forever on the lips of Russian statesmen, no longer sounded true in the meridian of Tokio.

The ruler of Japan had not offered me so much as a yen. Nay, it was clearly expected and intended that I should devote myself to the service of my new country without pay, and with the same single-hearted devotion as Mr. Katahashi himself. The Mikado was going to enroll in his services as an unpaid volunteer the most highly-paid, in other words, the most trusted and feared, secret service agent of two hemispheres.

And it was to cost him? An embroidered garment and two sentences spoken in a private audience!

Such are the methods of Japan!

On our arrival at the Palace we were received by a chamberlain, who conducted us by the private staircase to the Hall of the Imperial Family.

The Hall is an imposing room, hung with portraits of deceased mikados. A single chair, decorated with the emblem of the Rising Sun, stood at the upper end.

Almost as soon as we had taken our places, a door behind the chair was thrown up, and a number of the officers of the household, all wearing the ancient national costume, filed in, and grouped themselves around the imperial chair.

Then a silver bell sounded, and his imperial and sacred majesty, Mutsuhito CXXI., Mikado, walked slowly forward into the Hall, accompanied by his son and heir, the Crown Prince Yoshihito, and an elderly man, attired with great richness, who was, as my guide whispered to me, his imperial highness Prince Yorimo, second cousin to the Emperor, and the man who had consented to be my titular father.

The ceremony was brief but impressive. I could not but be struck by the contrast between the two Mikados—the one whom I had seen yesterday, an alert statesman, wearing Western clothes, and speaking French with hardly a trace of accent, and the one before me now, a solemn, pontifical figure, in his immemorial robes, moving, speaking with the etiquette of a bygone age.

Everything passed in the Japanese language, of which I did not then know a single word.

Mr. Katahashi did his best to provide a running translation, whispering in my ear, and prompting me with the Japanese words which it was necessary for me to pronounce.

As far as I could understand, Prince Yorimo asked permission of the Emperor to adopt a son, as he was childless and desired to have some one who would sacrifice to his own spirit and those of his father and grandfather after he was dead.

The Mikado graciously consenting, I was brought forward, and made to renounce my own family and ancestors, and promise to sacrifice exclusively to those of my new father.

Prince Yorimo next brought forward a robe embroidered with the imperial emblems, the most prominent of which was the Rising Sun. I was divested of the dress lent me by Katahashi, and my adoptive father flung the imperial garment over my shoulders.

The girding on of the samurai weapon followed, and my father addressed me a short exhortation, bidding me hold myself ready at all times to obey the will of the Divine Emperor, even to the point of committing *seppuku* at his command.

Seppuku is the correct name of the rite known in the West by the vulgar name of *hara-kiri*, or the "happy despatch." It is a form of voluntary execution permitted by the ancient laws of Japan to men of noble rank, much as European nobles were allowed to be beheaded instead of being hanged.

I was then permitted to kiss the hand of Prince Yorimo, who formally presented me to the Mikado, whose hand also I had to kiss, kneeling.

That was the whole of the ceremony, at the close of which Mr. Katahashi bade me a temporary farewell, and my princely father carried me off to a banquet in his own mansion.

Tedious and uninteresting as I fear these details must seem to the reader, I have thought it right to record them as an illustration of the spirit of Japan, of that country of which I am proud to be an adopted son.

The moment we had quitted the Hall of the Imperial Family, Prince Yorimo began to talk to me in French.

He proved to be a most fascinating companion. Old enough to remember the feudal age, which was still in full vigor in Japan forty years ago, he had since mastered most of the knowledge of the West.

I soon found that the Prince was by no means disposed to treat the adoption as a mere form. It was evident that the old gentleman had taken a strong fancy to me. He gave me a most affectionate welcome on the threshold of his house, and immediately calling his servants around him, introduced me to them as their future master, and bade them obey me as himself.

I was more touched than I care to say by this kind treatment. My own parents have long been dead; I know nothing of any other relations, if I have any; I have long been a wanderer and an adventurer on the face of the earth, and now, at last, I felt as though I had found a home.

Something of this I tried to convey to his imperial highness.

"My son," he replied with deep tenderness, "I feel that to me you will be a son indeed. You shall learn the language of our beautiful country, you shall grow used to our national ways. Before long you will let me provide you with a daughter of the Chrysanthemum to be your wife, and my grandchildren shall be Japanese indeed."

A sound of bells was heard outside.

"My friends are coming to pay the customary congratulation," the aged prince explained. "As it is necessary that you should have a name suited to your new rank, I ask you to take that of my father, Matsukata."

A few words of direction were spoken to the steward of the chambers, who went out. Immediately afterward he returned, throwing open the doors widely, and announced:

"The Marquis Yamagata to congratulate his imperial highness Prince Matsukata!"

And the Prime Minister of Japan came toward me.

Chapter 14 The Submarine Mine

Having told the reader as much as was necessary to enable him to understand my subsequent proceedings, and the real forces at work in the underground struggle which produced the tragedy of the Dogger Bank, I will suppress the remainder of my adventures in Tokio.

When I left the capital of my new country I wore around my neck, under the light shirt of chain mail without which I have never traveled for the last twenty years, a golden locket containing the miniature portrait of the loveliest maiden in the East or in the West.

It was a pledge. When little, tender fingers had fastened it in its place, little moving lips had whispered in my ear, "Till peace is signed!"

I had decided to return to the capital of what was now the country of my enemies, by much the same route as I had left it.

To do so, it was necessary to run the blockade of Port Arthur, or rather to feign to do so, for the Japanese Minister of Marine had been asked by my friend Katahashi to give secret instructions to Admiral Togo on my behalf.

In order to ensure a welcome from the Russian commander, and to dispel any suspicions, I planned to take in a cargo of Welsh steam coal.

Through an agent at Yokohama I chartered a British collier lying at Chi-fu, with a cargo for disposal. Leaving the Japanese port on a steamer bound for Shanghai, I met the collier in mid-ocean, and transferred myself on board her.

As soon as I had taken command, I ordered the skipper to head for Port Arthur.

This was the first intimation to him that he was expected to run the blockade, and at first he refused.

"I'm not afraid—myself," the sturdy Briton declared, "but I've got a mixed crew on board, Germans and Norwegians and Lascars, and all sorts, and I can't rely on them if we get in a tight place."

I glanced around at the collection of foreign faces and drew the captain aside. He, at least, was an Englishman, and I therefore trusted him.

"There is no danger, really," I said. "Admiral Togo has had secret orders to let me through. This cargo is merely a pretext."

The rough sailor scratched his head.

"Well, maybe you're telling the truth," he grunted. "But, dang me, if I can get the hang of it. You might belong to any country almost by the cut of your jib; you say you've fixed things up with the blessed Japs, and you're running a cargo of coal for the blessed Rooshians. It's queer, mortal queer, that's all I can say. Howsomdever——"

I took out a flask of three-star brandy, and passed it to the doubting mariner.

He put it first to his nose, then to his lips.

"Ah! Nothing wrong about that, Mister," he pronounced, as he handed back the flask.

"It's a fifty-pound job for yourself, no matter what becomes of the cargo," I insinuated.

The worthy seaman's manner underwent a magic change.

"Port your helm!" he yelled out suddenly and sharply to the man at the wheel. "Keep her steady nor'-east by nor', and a point nor'. Full steam ahead! All lights out! And if one of you lubbers so much as winks an eyelid, by George, I'll heave him overboard!"

The crew, who had shown a good many signs of uneasiness since my coming over the side, seemed to think this last hint worth attending to. They slunk forward to their duties, leaving the captain and myself to pace the quarter-deck alone.

We steamed swiftly through the darkness till we began to see the search-lights of the Japanese fleet like small white feathers fluttering on the horizon.

"Come up on the bridge," the skipper advised. "Got a revolver handy?"

I showed him my loaded weapon.

"Right! I ain't much afraid of the Japs, but we may have trouble with some of that all-sorts crew I've got below."

By and by the white plumes became bigger. All at once a ship lying dark on the water, scarcely a mile away on the weather-bow, spat out a long ribbon of light like an ant-eater's tongue, and we found ourselves standing in a glare of light as if we were actors in the middle of a stage.

There was a howl from below, and a mixed body of Lascars, headed by one of the Germans, rushed toward the helm.

"Back, you milk-drinking swabs!" the skipper roared. "As I'm a living man, the first one of you that lays a hand on the wheel, I'll fire into the crowd.

"Hark ye here!" their commander said with rough eloquence. "In the first place, it don't follow that because you can see a flashlight the chap at t'other end can see you. Second place, no ship that does see us is going to sink us without giving us a round of blank first, by way of notice to heave to. Third place, if we do get a notice, I'm going to stop this ship. And, fourth place, you've got five seconds to decide whether you'd rather be taken into Yokohama by a prize crew of Japs, or be shot where you stand by me and this gentleman."

The crew turned tail. Before five seconds had elapsed, not a head was to be seen above decks, except that of the man at the helm, who happened to be a Dane, to be first mate, and to be more than three-parts drunk.

Needless to say the warning shot was not fired.

We steamed steadily on through the fleet, every vessel of which was probably by this time aware of our presence. The search-lights flashed and fell all around us, but not once did we have to face again that blinking glare which tells the blockade runner that the game is up.

But there was another peril in store on which we had not reckoned. The sea all around Port Arthur had been strewn with Russian mines!

Unconscious of what was coming, we steamed gaily past the last outlying torpedo-boat of Admiral Togo's squadron.

"Through!" cried my friend the skipper, pointing with a grin of delight at the Port Arthur lights as they came into view around the edge of a dark cliff.

And even as he looked and pointed, there was a terrific wave, a rush, a flare and a report, and I felt myself lifted off my feet into mid-air.

I fancy I must have been unconscious for a second or two while in the air, for the splash of the sea as I struck it in falling seemed to wake me up like a cold douche.

My first movement, on coming to the surface again, was to put my hand to my neck to make sure of the safety of the precious locket which had been placed there by my dear little countrywoman.

My second was to strike out for a big spar which I saw floating amid a mass of tangled cordage and splinters a few yards in front of me.

Strange as it may seem, only when my arms were resting safely on the spar, and I had time to look about me and take stock of the situation, did I realize the extreme peril I had been in.

Most dangers and disasters are worse to read about than to go through. Had any one warned me beforehand that I was going to be blown up by a mine, I should probably have felt the keenest dread, and conjured up all sorts of horrors. As it was, the whole adventure was over in a twinkling, and by the greatest good luck I had escaped without a scratch.

By this time the forts at the entrance to Port Arthur, attracted, no doubt, by the noise of the explosion, were busily searching the spot with their lights.

The effect was truly magnificent.

From the blackness of the heights surrounding the famous basin, fiery sword after fiery sword seemed to leap forth and stab the sea. The wondrous blades of light met and crossed one another as if some great archangels were doing battle for the key of Asia.

The whole sea was lit up with a brightness greater than that of the sun. Every floating piece of wreckage, every rope, every nail stood out with unnatural clearness. I was obliged to close my eyes, and protect them with my dripping hand.

Presently I heard a hail from behind me. I turned my head, and to my delight saw the brave skipper of the lost ship swimming toward me.

In another dozen strokes he was alongside and clinging with me to the same piece of wood, which he said was the main gaff.

He was rather badly gashed about the head, but not enough to threaten serious consequences. So far as we could ascertain, the whole of the crew had perished.

I confess that their fate did not cost me any very great pang, after the first natural shock of horror had passed. They owed their death to their own lack of courage, which had caused them to take refuge in the lowest part of the ship, where the full force of the explosion came. The captain and I, thanks to our position on the bridge, had escaped with a comparatively mild shaking.

The steersman would have escaped also, in all probability, had he been sober.

In a very short time after the captain had joined me, our eyes were gladdened by the sight of a launch issuing from the fort to our assistance.

The officer in charge had thoughtfully provided blankets and a flask of wine. Thus comforted, I was not long in fully recovering my strength, and by the time the launch had set us on shore my comrade in misfortune was also able to walk without difficulty.

The lieutenant who had picked us up showed the greatest consideration on learning that we had been blown up in an attempt to run a cargo of coal for the benefit of the Russian fleet. On landing we were taken before Admiral Makharoff, the brave man whom fate had marked out to perish two months later by a closely similar catastrophe.

The story which I told to the Admiral was very nearly

true, though of course I suppressed the incidents which had taken place in Tokio.

I said that I had been charged to deliver a private communication from the Czar to the Mikado, sent in the hope of averting war, that I had arrived too late, and that, having to make my way back to Petersburg, I had meant to do a stroke of business on the way on behalf of his excellency.

My inspector's uniform, which I had resumed on leaving Yokohama, confirmed my words, and Admiral Makharoff, after thanking me on behalf of the navy for my zeal, dismissed me with a present of a thousand rubles, and a permit to travel inland from Port Arthur.

Needless to say I did not forget to say good-by to my brave Englishman, to whom I handed over the Russian Admiral's reward, thus doubling the amount I had promised him for his plucky stand against the mutineers.

I have hurried over these transactions, interesting as they were, in order to come to the great struggle which lay before me in the capital of Russia.

Chapter 15 *The Advisor of Nicholas II*

By the second week in March I was back in Petersburg.

On the long journey across Asia, I had had time to mature my plans, with the advantage of knowing that the real enemy I had to fight was neither M. Petrovitch nor the witching Princess Y——, but the Power which was using them both as its tools.

It was a frightful thing to know that two mighty peoples, the Japanese and Russians, neither of which really wished to fight each other, had been locked in strife in order to promote the sinister and tortuous policy of Germany.

So far, the German Kaiser had accomplished one-half of his program. The second, and more important, step would be to bring about a collision between the Russians and the English.

Thus the situation resolved itself into an underground duel between Wilhelm II. and myself, a duel in which the whole future history of the world, and possibly the very existence of the British Empire, hung in the balance.

And the arbiter was the melancholy young man who wandered through the vast apartments of his palace at Tsarskoe-Selo like some distracted ghost, wishing that any lot in life had been bestowed on him rather than that of autocrat of half Europe and Asia.

It was to Nicholas that I first repaired, on my return, to report the result of my mission.

I obtained a private audience without difficulty, and found his majesty busily engaged in going through some papers relating to the affairs of the Navy.

"So they have not killed you, like poor Menken," he said

with a mixture of sympathy and sadness.

"Colonel Menken killed!" I could not forbear exclaiming.

"Yes. Did you not hear of it? A Japanese spy succeeded in assassinating him, and stealing the despatch, just before Mukden. A lady-in-waiting attached to the Dowager Czaritza happened to be on the train, and brought me the whole story."

I shook my head gravely.

"I fear your majesty has been misinformed. Colonel Menken committed suicide. I saw him put the pistol to his head and shoot himself. His last words were a message to your majesty."

The Czar raised his hand to his head with a despairing gesture.

"Will these contradictions never end!" he exclaimed. "Really, sir, I hope you have made a mistake. Whom *can* I trust!"

I drew myself up.

"I have no desire to press my version on you, sire," I said coldly. "It is sufficient that the Colonel was robbed, and that he is dead. Perhaps Princess Y— — has also given you an account of my own adventures?"

Nicholas II. looked at me distrustfully.

"Let us leave the name of the Princess on one side," he said in a tone of rebuke. "I have every reason to feel satisfied with her loyalty and zeal."

I bowed, and remained silent.

"You failed to get through, I suppose," the Czar continued, after waiting in vain for me to speak.

"I beg pardon, sire, I safely delivered to the Emperor of Japan your majesty's autograph on the cigarette paper. I was robbed of the more formal letter in the house of M. Petrovitch, before starting."

Nicholas frowned.

"Petrovitch again! Another of the few men whom I know to be my real friends." He fidgeted impatiently.

"Well, what did the Mikado say?"

I had intended to soften the reply of the Japanese Emperor, but now, being irritated, I gave it bluntly:

"His majesty professed to disbelieve in your power to control your people. He declared that he could not treat a letter from you seriously unless you were able to send it openly, without your messengers being robbed or murdered on the way across your own dominions."

The young Emperor flushed darkly.

"Insolent barbarian!" he cried hotly. "The next letter I send him shall be delivered by the commander of my army on the soil of Japan."

I was secretly pleased by this flash of spirit, which raised my respect for the Russian monarch.

A recollection seemed to strike him.

"I hear that you were blown up in attempting to bring some coal into Port Arthur," he said in a more friendly tone. "I thank you, Monsieur V — —."

I bowed low.

"Some of my admirals seem to have been caught napping," Nicholas II. added. "I have here a very serious report about Admiral Stark at Vladivostok."

"You surprise me, sire," I observed incautiously. "Out in Manchuria I heard the Admiral praised on all hands for his carefulness and good conduct."

"Carefulness! It is possible to be too careful," the Czar

complained. "Admiral Stark is too much afraid of responsibility. We have information that the English are taking all kinds of contraband into the Japanese ports, and he does nothing to stop them, for fear of committing some breach of international law."

I began to see what was coming. The Emperor, who seemed anxious to justify himself, proceeded:

"The rights of neutrals have never been regarded by the British navy, when they were at war. However, I have not been satisfied with taking the opinion of our own jurists. I have here an opinion from Professor Heldenberg of Berlin, who of course represents a neutral Power, and he says distinctly that we are entitled to declare anything we please contraband, and to seize English ships—I mean, ships of neutrals—anywhere, even in the English Channel itself, and sink them if it is inconvenient to bring them into a Russian port."

The insidious character of this advice was so glaring that I wondered how the unfortunate young monarch could be deceived by it.

But I saw that comment would be useless just then. I must seek some other means of opening his eyes to the pitfalls which were being prepared for him.

I came from the Palace with a heavy heart. The next day, Petersburg was startled by the publication of a ukase recalling Vice-Admiral Stark and Rear-Admiral Molas, his second in command, from the Pacific.

Immediately on hearing this news I sent a telegram in cipher to Lord Bedale. For obvious reasons I never take copies of my secret correspondence, but to the best of my recollection the wire ran as follows:

Germany instigating Russian Navy to raid your shipping

on the pretext of contraband. Object to provoke reprisals leading to war.

As the reader is aware, this warning succeeded in defeating the Kaiser's main design, the British Government steadily refusing to be provoked.

Unfortunately this attitude of theirs played into German hands in another way, as English shippers were practically obliged to refuse goods for the Far East, and this important and lucrative trade passed to Hamburg, to the serious injury of the British ports.

But before this development had been reached, I found myself on the track of a far more deadly and dangerous intrigue, one which is destined to live in history as the most audacious plot ever devised by one great Power against another with which it proposed to be on terms of perfect friendship.

Chapter 16 A Strange Confession

I had last seen the strange, beautiful, wicked woman known as the Princess Y— — bending in a passion of hysterical remorse over the body of the man she had driven to death, on the snow-clad train outside Mukden.

I have had some experience of women, and especially of the class which mixes in the secret politics of the European Courts. But Sophia Y— — was an enigma to me. There was nothing about her which suggested the adventuress. And there was much which tended to support the story which had won the belief of her august mistress—that she was an involuntary agent, who had been victimized by an unscrupulous minister of police, by means of a false charge, and who genuinely loathed the tasks she was too feeble to refuse.

I had not been back in Petersburg very long when one afternoon the hotel waiter came to tell me that a lady desired to see me privately. The lady, he added, declined to give her name, but declared that she was well known to me.

I had come back to the hotel, I should mention, in the character of Mr. Sterling, the self-appointed agent of the fraternity of British peace-makers. It was necessary for me to have some excuse for residing in Petersburg during the war, and under this convenient shelter I could from time to time prepare more effectual disguises.

I was not altogether surprised when my mysterious visitor raised her veil and disclosed the features of the Princess herself.

But I was both surprised and shocked by the frightened, grief-stricken look on the face of this woman whom I had come to dread as my most formidable opponent in the Russian Court.

"Mr. Sterling!—Monsieur V——?" she cried in an agitated voice that seemed ready to break down into a sob. "Can you forgive me for intruding on you? I dare not speak to you freely in my own house. I am beset by spies."

"Sit down, Princess," I said soothingly, as I rolled forward a comfortable chair. "Of course I am both charmed and flattered by your visit, whatever be its cause."

With feminine intuition she marked the reserve in my response to her appeal.

"Ah! You distrust me, and you are quite right!" she exclaimed, casting herself into the chair.

She fixed her luminous eyes on me in a deep look, half-imploring, half-reproachful.

"It is true, then, what they have been telling me? You were the man, dressed as an inspector of the Third Section who traveled on the train with me? And you saw the death"—her words were interrupted by a shudder—"of that unhappy man?"

It was not very easy to preserve my composure in the face of her emotion. Nevertheless, at the risk of appearing callous, I replied:

"I cannot pretend to understand your question. However, even if I did it would make no difference.

"Since you know my name is A. V——, you must know also that I never allow myself to talk about my work."

The Princess winced under these cold words almost as though she had been physically rebuffed. She clasped her delicately-gloved hands together, and murmured as though to herself:

"He will not believe in me! He will not be convinced!"

I felt myself in a very difficult position. Either this woman was thoroughly repentant, and sincerely anxious to make some genuine communication to me, or else she was an actress whose powers might have excited envy in the Bernhardt herself.

I concluded that I could lose nothing by encouraging her to speak.

"You must pardon me if I seem distrustful," I said with a wholly sympathetic expression. "I have my principles, and cannot depart from them. But I have every wish to convince you of my personal friendship."

She interrupted me with a terrible glance.

"Personal friendship! Monsieur, do you know what I have come here to tell you?"

And rising wildly to her feet, she spread out her hands in a gesture of utter despair:

"They have ordered me to take your life!"

I am not a man who is easily surprised.

The adventures I have passed through, some of them far more extraordinary than anything I have recorded in my public revelations, have accustomed me to meet almost any situation with diplomatic presence of mind.

But on this occasion I am obliged to admit that I was fairly taken aback.

As the lovely but dangerous woman whom I had cause to regard as the most formidable instrument in the hands of the conspirators, avowed to my face that she had been charged with the mission to assassinate me, I sprang from my chair and confronted her.

She stood, swaying slightly, as though the intensity of her emotion was about to overpower her.

"Do you mean what you say? Do you know what you have said?" I demanded.

The Princess Y— — made no answer, but she lifted her violet eyes to mine, and I saw the big tears welling up and beginning to overflow.

I was dismayed. My strength of mind seemed to desert me. I have looked on without a tear when men have fallen dead at my feet, but I have never been able to remain calm before a woman in tears.

"Madame! Princess!" I was on the point of addressing her by a yet more familiar name. "At least, sit down and recover yourself."

Like one dazed, I led her to a chair. Like one dazed, she sank into it in obedience to my authoritative pressure.

"Come," I said in a tone which I strove to render at once firm and soothing, "it is clear that we must understand each other. You have come here to tell me this, I suppose?"

"At the risk of my life," she breathed. "What must you think of me!"

I recalled the fate of poor Menken, whom the woman before me had led to his doom, though she had not struck the blow.

In spite of myself, a momentary shudder went through me.

The sensitive woman saw or felt it, and shook in her turn.

"Believe me or not, as you will," she exclaimed desperately. "I swear to you that I have never knowingly been guilty of taking life.

"Never for one moment did I anticipate that that poor man would do what he did," the Princess went on with passionate earnestness. "I tempted him to give me the Czar's letter, and I destroyed it—I confess that. Are not such things done every day in secret politics? Have you never intercepted a despatch?"

It was a suggestive question. I thought of more than one incident in my own career which might be harshly received by a strict moralist. It is true that I have always been engaged on what I believed was a lawful task; but the due execution of that task had sometimes involved actions which I should have shrunk from in private life.

"I will not excuse myself, Madame," I answered slowly. "Neither have I accused you."

"Your tone is an accusation," she returned with a touch of bitterness. "Oh, I know well that men are ready to pardon many things in one another which they will not pardon in us."

"I am sorry if I have wounded you," I said with real compunction. "Let us say no more about the tragedy that is past. Am I right in thinking that you have come to me for aid?"

"I do not know. I do not know why I am here. Perhaps it is because I am mad."

I gazed at her flushed face and trembling hands, unable to resist the feeling of compassion which was creeping over me.

What was I to think? What was this woman's real purpose in coming to me?

Had her employers, had the unscrupulous Petrovitch, or the ruthless Minister of Police, indeed charged her to remove me from their path; and had her courage broken down under the hideous burden?

Or was this merely a ruse to win my confidence; or, perhaps, to frighten me into resigning my task and leaving the

Russian capital?

Did she wish to save my life, or her own?

I sat regarding her, bewildered by these conjectures.

I saw that I must get her to say more.

"At least you have come to aid me," I protested. "You have given me a warning for which I cannot be sufficiently grateful."

"If you believe it is a genuine one," she retorted. Already she had divined my difficulties and doubts.

"I do not doubt that you mean it genuinely," I hastened to respond. "There is, of course, the possibility that you yourself have been deceived."

"Ah!"

She looked up at me in what I could not think was other than real surprise.

"You think so?" she cried eagerly. The next moment her head drooped again. "No, no. I have known them too long. They have never trifled with me before. Believe me, Monsieur, when they told me that you were to be murdered they were not joking with me."

"But they might have meant to use you for the purpose of terrifying me."

She stared at me in unaffected astonishment.

"Terrify—*you*!" She pronounced the words with an emphasis not altogether unflattering. "You are better known in Russia than you imagine, M. V——."

I passed over the remark.

"Still they must have foreseen the possibility that you would shrink from such a task; that your womanly instincts would prove too much for you. At least they have never required such work of you before?"

Against my will the last words became a question. I was anxious to be assured that the hands of the Princess were free from the stain of blood.

"Never! They dared not! They *could* not!" she cried indignantly. "You do not know my history. Perhaps you do not care to know it?"

Whatever I knew or suspected, I could make only one answer to such an appeal. Indeed, I was desirous to understand the meaning of one word which the Princess Y—— had just used.

"Listen," she said, speaking with an energy and dignity which I could not but respect, "while I tell you what I am. I am a condemned murderess!"

"Impossible!"

"Impossible in any other country, I grant you, but very possible in Russia. You have heard, I suppose, everybody has heard, of the deaths of my husband and his children. The first two deaths were natural, I swear it. I, at all events, had no more to do with them than if they had occurred in the planet Saturn. Prince Y—— committed suicide. And he did so because of me; I do not deny it. But it was not because he suspected me of any hand in the deaths of his children. It was because he knew I hated him!

"The story is almost too terrible to be told. That old man had bought me. He bought me from my father, who was head over ears in debt, and on the brink of ruin. I was sold—the only portion of his property that remained to be sold. And from the first hour of the purchase I hated, oh, how I loathed and hated that old man!"

There was a wild note in her voice that hinted at unutterable things.

"And he," she continued with a shiver, "he loved me, loved me with a passion that was like madness. He could hardly bear me out of his sight.

"I killed him, yes, morally, I have no doubt I killed him. He lavished everything on me, jewels, wealth, all the forms of luxury. He made a will leaving me the whole of his great fortune. But I could not endure him, and that killed him. I think," she hesitated and lowered her voice to a whisper, "I think he killed himself to please me."

Hardened as I am, I felt a thrill of horror. The Princess was right; the story was too terrible to be told.

"Then the police came on the scene. From the first they knew well enough that I was innocent. But they were determined to make me guilty. The head of the secret service at that time was Baron Kratz. He had had his eye on me for some time. The Czar, believing in my guilt, had ordered him not to spare me, and that fatal order gave him a free hand.

"How he managed it all, I hardly know. The servants were bullied or bribed into giving false evidence against me. But one part of their evidence was true enough; even I could not deny that I had hated Prince Y——, and that his death came as a welcome relief.

"There was a secret trial, and I was condemned. They read out my sentence. And then, when it was all over, Kratz came to me, and offered me life and liberty in return for my services as an agent of the Third Section."

"And to save your life you consented. Well, I do not judge you," I said.

The Princess glanced at me with a strange smile.

"To save my life! I see you do not yet know our Holy Russia. Shall I tell you what my sentence was?"

"Was it not death, then?"

"Yes, death—by the knout!"

"My God!"

I gazed at her stupified. Her whole beauty seemed to be focussed in one passionate protest. Knouted to death! I saw the form before me stripped, and lashed to the triangles, while the knotted thong, wielded by the hangman's hands, buried itself in the soft flesh.

I no longer disbelieved. I no longer even doubted. The very horror of the story had the strength of truth.

For some time neither of us spoke.

"But now, surely, you have made up your mind to break lose from this thraldom?" I demanded. "And, if so, and you will trust me, I will undertake to save you."

"You forget, do you not, that you yourself are not free? You surely do not mean that you would lay aside your work for my sake?"

It was a question which disconcerted me in more ways than one. In a secret service agent, suspicion becomes second nature. I caught myself asking whether all that had gone before was not merely intended to lead up to this one question, and I cursed myself for the doubt.

"My duty to my present employer comes first, of course," I admitted. "But as soon as I am free again——"

"If you are still alive," she put in significantly.

"Ah! You mean?"

"I mean that when they find out that I am not to be

depended on, they will not have far to look for others."

"It is strange that they should have chosen you in the first place," I said thoughtfully. "You said they *could* not ask you."

"They did not offer me this mission. I volunteered."

"You volunteered!"

She shook herself impatiently.

"Surely you understand? I heard them deciding on your death. And so I undertook the task."

"Because?"

"Because I wished to save you. I had great difficulty. At first they were inclined to refuse me—to suspect my motives. I had to convince them that I hated you for having outwitted me. And I persuaded them that none of their ordinary instruments were capable of dealing with you."

"And you meant to give me this warning all along?"

"I meant to save you from them. Do you not see, as long as we are together, as long as you are visiting me, and I am seen to be following you up, they will not interfere. If I manage the affair skilfully it may be weeks before they suspect that I am playing them false. I shall have my excuse ready. It is no disgrace to be foiled by A. V."

Again there was an interval of silence. The Princess prepared to go.

"Stay!" I protested. "I have not thanked you. Indeed, I do not seem to have heard all. You had some reason, surely, for wishing to preserve my life."

"And what does my reason matter?"

"It matters very much to me. Perhaps," I gave her a searching look, "perhaps the Dowager Czaritza has enlisted you on our side?"

The beautiful woman rose to her feet, and turned her face from me.

"Think so, if you will. I tell you it does not matter."

"And I tell you it does matter. Princess!"

"Don't! Don't speak to me, please! Let me go home. I am not well."

Trembling violently in every limb, she was making her way toward the door, when it was suddenly flung open, and the voice of the hotel servant announced:

"M. Petrovitch!"

The head of the Manchurian Syndicate walked in with a smile on his face, saw the Princess Y—— coming toward him, and stopped short, the smile changing to a dark frown.

Chapter 17 A Supernatural Incident

Whether because he saw that I was watching him, or because he placed his own interpretation on the circumstances, the war plotter changed his frown into a smile.

"I am glad to see, Princess," he said to the trembling woman, "that you have so soon found our good friend Mr. Sterling again."

The Princess Y— — gave him a glance which seemed to enjoin silence, bowed with grace, and left the room in charge of the servant who had announced M. Petrovitch.

The latter now advanced to greet me with every appearance of cordiality.

The last time I had met this well-dressed, delicate scamp, he had drugged and robbed me. Now I had just been told that he was setting assassins on my track.

But it is my rule always to cultivate friendly intercourse with my opponents. Few men can talk for long without exposing something of their inner thoughts. I wanted M. Petrovitch to talk.

Therefore I returned his greeting with equal cordiality, and made him sit down in the chair from which the Princess Y — — had just risen.

"You will be surprised to hear, no doubt, Mr. Sterling, that I have brought you an invitation from the Emperor."

"From what Emperor?" was the retort on the tip of my tongue. Fortunately I suppressed it; there is no accomplishment so fatal to success in life as wit, except kindness.

I simply answered,

"I am not readily surprised, M. Petrovitch. Neither, I

imagine, are you."

The financier smiled.

"May I call you M. V——?" he asked. "His majesty has told me who you are."

"Were you surprised by that?" I returned with sarcasm.

Petrovitch fairly laughed.

"I hear you have been denouncing me to Nicholas," he said lightly. "Can't I persuade you to let our poor little Czar alone. I assure you it is a waste of breath on your part, and you will only worry a well-meaning young man who has no head for business."

This was plain speaking. It argued no ordinary confidence on the part of the intriguer to speak in such a fashion of the Autocrat of All the Russias.

Already the interview was telling me something. Petrovitch must have some strong, secret hold on Nicholas II.

I shrugged my shoulders as I answered in my friendliest manner,

"I have no personal feeling against you, my dear Petrovitch. But to use drugs—come, you must admit that that was a strong measure!"

"I apologize!" laughed the Russian. "All the more as I find you were too many for us after all. I would give something to know how you managed to hide the letter you got through."

It was my turn to laugh. I had reason to feel satisfied. Weak as the Russian Emperor might be, it was evident that he had not betrayed my secret.

"Well, now," the promoter resumed, "all that being over, is there any reason why we should not be friends? Be frank with me. What end have you in view that is likely to bring us into collision?"

"There is no reason why I should not be frank with you," I answered, racking my brain for some story which the man before me might be likely to believe, "especially as I do not suppose that either of us is likely to report this conversation quite faithfully to his imperial majesty. I am a Japanese spy."

Petrovitch gave me a glance in which I thought I detected a mingling of incredulity and admiration.

"Really, you are a cool hand, my dear V——!"

"Why, is there anything in that to make us enemies? You are not going to pose as the zealous patriot, I hope. I thought we had agreed to be frank."

The financier bit his lip.

"Well, I do not deny that I am before all things a man of business," he returned. "If your friends the Japanese can make me any better offer than the one I have had from another quarter, I do not say."

"I will see what I can arrange for you," I answered, not wholly insincerely. "In the meantime, I think you said something about an invitation?"

"Oh, yes, from Nicholas. He wants to see you. He has some scheme or other in which he thinks that you and I can work together, and he wants us to be friends, accordingly."

"But we are friends, after to-day, I understand?"

"It is as you please, my dear V——," replied the conspirator with a slightly baffled air. "You have made a good beginning, apparently, with the Princess Y——."

I put on the self-satisfied air of the man who is a favorite with women.

"The Princess has been extremely kind," I said. "She has

pressed me to visit her frequently. Oh, yes, I think I may say we are good friends."

Petrovitch nodded. I had purposely prepared his mind for the story which I anticipated he would hear from my beautiful protector. Evidently it would be necessary for her to tell the Syndicate that she was feigning affection for me in order to draw me into a trap.

"Then, as my carriage is outside, may I take you to the Winter Palace?"

"That seems the best plan," I acquiesced. "It will convince the Czar that we are on good terms."

We drove off together, sitting side by side like two sworn friends. I do not know what thoughts passed through his mind; but I know that all the way I kept my right hand on the stock of my revolver, and once, when one of the horses stumbled, M. Petrovitch was within an instant of death.

At the Palace he put me down and drove off. I was admitted to the Czar's presence without difficulty, and found him, as usual, surrounded by piles of state papers.

Nicholas II. looked up at my entrance with evident pleasure.

"Ah, that is right, M. V— —. I hope that, since you have come so promptly in response to the message I gave that worthy M. Petrovitch, you and he are now good friends."

I could only bow silently. I was a Japanese, related to the sovereign with whom he was at war, and I was acting in the service of Great Britain. Petrovitch had just forced on the war which Nicholas had wished to avert, and he was still acting secretly in the interests of Germany. And the Czar was congratulating himself that we were friends. It was useless to try to undeceive him.

"Sit down, if you please, M. V— —. I have something of the greatest importance to tell you. Stay—Perhaps you will be good enough to see first that the doors are all secured. I dislike interruptions."

I went to the various entrances of the room, of which there were three, and turned the keys in the doors.

"Even M. Petrovitch does not know what I am going to tell you," Nicholas said impressively as I returned to my seat.

"Your majesty does not trust him entirely, then?" I exclaimed, much pleased.

"You mistake me. I do not distrust M. Petrovitch; but this is a matter of foreign politics, with which he is not familiar. He admits frankly that he knows nothing about diplomacy."

I gazed at the benevolent young monarch in consternation. It was the spy of Wilhelm II., the agent of the most active diplomatist in the world, of whom he had just spoken!

There was no more to be said.

The Emperor proceeded to put a most unexpected question.

"Are you a believer in spirits, M. V— —?"

"I am a Roman Catholic, sire. Whatever my Church teaches on this subject, I believe. I am rather neglectful of my religious duties, however, and do not know its attitude on this subject."

"I honor your loyalty to your communion, M. V— —. But as long as you do not know what is the attitude of your Church on this subject, you cannot feel it wrong to listen to me."

I perceived that if his majesty was no politician, he was at least something of a theologian.

The Czar proceeded:

"There is in Petersburg one of the most marvelous mediums and clairvoyants who has ever lived. He is a Frenchman named Auguste. He came here nearly a year ago—just when the difficulty with Japan was beginning, in fact; and he has given me the most valuable information about the progress of events. Everything he has foretold has come true, so far. He warned me from the first that the Japanese would force me into war, just as they have done. In short, I feel I can rely on him absolutely."

This was not the first time I had heard of the spiritualist who had established such an extraordinary hold on the Russian ruler's mind. The common impression was that he was a mystic, a sort of Madame Krüdener. At the worst he was regarded as a charlatan of the ordinary spirit-rapping type, cultivating the occult as a means of making money.

But now, as I listened to the credulous monarch, it suddenly struck me what an invaluable tool such a man might prove in the hands of a political faction, or even of a foreign Power astute enough to corrupt him and inspire the oracles delivered by the spirits.

I listened anxiously for more.

The Emperor, evidently pleased with the serious expression on my face, went on to enlighten me.

"Last night M. Auguste was here, in this room, and we held a private *séance*. He succeeded in getting his favorite spirit to respond."

"Is it permissible to ask the spirit's name?" I ventured respectfully.

"It is Madame Blavatsky," he answered. "You must have

heard of her, of course. She was practically the founder of rational psychical knowledge, though she died a victim to persecution."

I nodded. I had heard of this celebrated woman, who still numbers many followers in different parts of the world.

"Last night, as soon as we found that the spirit of Madame Blavatsky was present, I asked Auguste to question it about the Baltic fleet.

"I had been holding a preliminary review of the fleet in the morning, as you may have seen from the papers. The officers and men seemed thoroughly nervous, and very doubtful whether it would ever be in a condition to sail. Even the Admiral, Rojestvensky, did not seem quite happy, and he found great fault with the stores and equipments.

"I had to authorize a delay of another month, and the Marine Department would not promise to have the fleet ready even then.

"Naturally, I wished to know what would become of the fleet when it did sail. Auguste questioned the spirit."

His majesty broke off to feel in his pocket for a small slip of paper.

"I took down the answer myself, as the spirit rapped it out." And he read aloud:

Baltic Fleet threatened. Japanese and English plotting to destroy it on the way to Port Arthur.

I started indignantly.

"And you believe that, sire! You believe that the British Government, which has been straining every nerve to maintain peace, is capable of planning some secret outrage against your Navy?"

"It does not say the Government," he announced with satisfaction. "The spirit only warns me against the English. Private Englishmen are capable of anything. At this very moment, two Englishmen are arranging to run a torpedo boat secretly out of the Thames, disguised as a yacht, and to bring her to Libau for us."

This piece of information silenced me. It was no doubt possible that there might be Englishmen daring enough to assist the Japanese in some secret enterprise against a Russian fleet. But I felt I should like to have some better authority for the fact than the word of Madame Blavatsky's spirit.

"The warning is a very vague one, sire," I hinted.

"True. But I hope to receive a more definite message to-morrow night. I was going to ask you if you would have any objection to be present. You might then be able to put pressure on the British Government to prevent this crime."

Needless to say I accepted the imperial invitation with eagerness.

And I retired to send the following despatch to Lord Bedale:

When Baltic Fleet starts prepare for trouble. Have all ports watched. It is believed here that attack on it is preparing in England.

Who was M. Auguste?

This was the question that kept my mind busy after my singular interview with the Russian Emperor.

In accordance with my rule to avoid as much as possible mentioning the names of the humbler actors in the international drama, I have given the notorious medium a name which conceals his true one.

He appeared to be a foreigner, and the Czar's weakness in this direction was too well known for his patronage of the quack to excite much attention; apparently it had occurred to no one but myself that such a man might be capable of meddling in politics.

In his more public performances, so far as I could learn, the revelations of the spirits were confined to more harmless topics, such as the nature of the future state, or the prospect of an heir being born to the Russian crown.

In my quest for further light on this remarkable personage, my thoughts naturally turned to the Princess Y——.

I have not concealed that at our first meeting the charming collaborator of M. Petrovitch had made a very strong impression on me. Her subsequent conduct had made me set a guard on myself, and the memory of the Japanese maiden whose portrait had become my cherished "mascot," of course insured that my regard for the Princess could never pass the bounds of platonic friendship.

But the strange scene of the day before had moved me profoundly. Vanity is not a failing of which I am ever likely to be accused by my worst detractor, yet it was impossible for me to shut my eyes or ears to the confession which had been made with equal eloquence by the looks, the blushes and even the words of the beautiful Russian.

Was ever situation more stupid in all the elements of tragedy! This unhappy woman, spurred to all kinds of desperate deeds by the awful fear of the knout, had been overcome by that fatal power which has wrecked so many careers.

In the full tide of success, in the very midst of a life and death combat with the man it was her business to outwit and defeat, she had succumbed to love for him.

And now, to render her painful situation tenfold more painful, she was holding the dagger at his breast as the only means of keeping it out of the clutch of some more murderous hand.

Had I the pen of a romancer I might enlarge on this sensational theme. But I am a man of action, whose business it is to record facts, not to comment on them.

I sought the mansion on the Nevsky Prospect, and asked to see its mistress.

Evidently the visit was expected. The groom of the chambers—if that was his proper description—led me up-stairs, and into a charming boudoir.

A fire replenished by logs of sandalwood was burning in a malachite stove, and diffusing a dream-like fragrance through the chamber. The walls of the room were panelled in ivory, and the curtains that hung across the window frames were of embroidered silk and gold. Each separate chair and toy-like table was a work of art—ebony, cinnamon, and other rare and curious woods having been employed.

But the rarest treasure there was the mistress of all this

luxury. The inmate of the sumptuous prison, for such it truly was, lay back on a leopard-skin couch, set in the frame of a great silver sea-shell.

She had dressed for my coming in the quaint but gorgeous costume of ancient Russia, the costume worn by imperial usage at high State functions like coronations, weddings and christenings.

The high coif above her forehead flamed with jewels, and big, sleepy pearls slid and fell over her neck and bosom.

At my entrance she gave a soft cry, and raised herself on one white arm. I stepped forward as though I were a courtier saluting a queen, and pressed my lips to her extended hand.

"I expected you, Andreas."

Only two women in my life have I ever allowed to call me by my Christian name. One was the ill-starred lady who perished in the Konak in Belgrade. The other—but of her I may not speak.

But it was not for me to stand on ceremony with the woman who had interposed herself as a shield between me and the enemies who sought my death.

"You knew that I should come to thank you," I said.

"I do not wish for thanks," she answered, with a look that was more expressive than words. "I wish only that you should regard me as a friend."

"And in what other light is it possible for me to regard you, dear Princess?" I returned. "Only this friendship must not be all on one side. You, too, must consent to think of me as something more than a stranger whose life you have saved."

"Can you doubt that I have done so for a long time?"

It needed the pressure of the locket against my neck to

keep me from replying to this tenderly-spoken sentiment in a way which might have led to consequences, for the Russian Empire as well as for the Princess and myself, very different to those which have actually flowed from our conjunction.

Conquering my impulses as I best could, I sought for a reply which would not wear the appearance of a repulse.

"You misunderstand me," I said, putting on an expression of pride. "You little know the character of Andreas V— — if you think he can accept the humiliating position of the man who is under obligation to a woman—an obligation which he has done nothing to discharge. Not until I can tell myself that I have done something to place me on a higher level in your eyes, can my thoughts concerning you be happy ones."

A shade of disappointment passed over Sophia's face. She made a pettish gesture.

"Does not—friendship do away with all sense of obligation?" she complained.

"Not with me," I answered firmly. "No, Sophia, if you really care for me—for my friendship—you must let me do what I have sworn to do ever since I first saw you and heard some rumors of your tragic story."

"You mean?"

"You must let me break your odious bondage. I can deliver you, if you will only trust me, from the power of the Russian police, or any other power, and set you free to live the life of fascination and happiness which ought to be yours."

The Princess seemed plunged in meditation. At length she looked up— —

"You would undertake a hopeless task, my dear Andreas. Not even you can fathom all the ramifications of the intrigues in which I find myself an indispensable puppet. Those who control my movements will never let go the strings by which they hold me, and least of all, just now."

I was distressed to see that the Princess was disposed to evade my appeal for confidence. I answered with a slightly wounded air:

"I may know more than you think, more even than you know yourself on certain points. But of course you are not willing to confide in me fully — — "

"There can be no perfect trust without perfect" — The Princess, who spoke this sentence in Russian, concluded it with a word which may mean either friendship or love according to circumstances. As she pronounced it, it seemed like love.

"There can be no perfect love without perfect trust," I responded quickly, striving to assume the manner of an exacting lover.

And then, a happy thought striking me, I added in an aggrieved voice,

"Do you think it is nothing to me that you should be associated with other men in the most secret enterprises, holding private conferences with them, receiving them in your house, perhaps visiting them in theirs; that you should appear to be on intimate terms with the Grand Duke Staniolanus, with M. Petrovitch, with a man like this M. Auguste — — "

At the sound of this last name, to which I had artfully led up, Sophia sprang into a sitting posture and gave me a look of anger and fear.

"Who told you anything about M. Auguste?" she demanded in hoarse tones. "What has he to do with me?"

"Nay, it is not you who ought to ask me that," I returned.

"You may be a believer in his conjuring tricks, for aught I know. He may be more to you than a comrade, or even a prophet— more to you than I."

"Who told you that he was my comrade, as you call it?" the Princess insisted, refusing to be diverted from her point.

"No one," I said quite truthfully. "I should be glad to know that he was only that. But it is natural for me to feel some jealousy of all your friends."

The Princess appeared relieved by this admission. But this relief confirmed all my suspicions. I now felt certain that the medium was an important figure in the plot which I was trying to defeat. I saw, moreover, that however genuine my beautiful friend might be in her love for me and her desire to save my life, she had no intention of betraying the secrets of her fellow conspirators.

Her character presented an enigma almost impossible to solve. Perhaps it is not the part of a wise man ever to try to understand a woman. Her motives must always be mysterious, even to herself. It is sufficient if one can learn to forecast her actions, and even that is seldom possible.

"Then you refuse my help?" I asked reproachfully.

"You cannot help me," was the answer. "At least, that is, unless you possess some power I have no idea of at present."

It was an ingenious turning of the tables. Instead of my questioning the Princess, she was questioning me, in effect.

I made what was perhaps a rash admission.

"I am not wholly powerless, at all events. There are few sovereigns in Europe whom I have not obliged at some time or other. Even the German Emperor, though I have more than once crossed his path in public matters, is my personal friend. In spite of his occasional political errors, he is a stainless gentleman in private life, and I am sure he would hear with horror of your position and the means by which you had been forced into it."

Sophia looked at me with an expression of innocent bewilderment which I could scarcely believe to be real.

"The German Emperor! But what has he to do with me?"

"He is said to have some influence with the Czar," I said drily.

My companion bit her lip.

"Oh, the Czar!" Her tone was scathing in its mixture of pity and indifference. "Every one has some influence with the Czar. But is there any one with whom Nicholas has influence?"

It was the severest thing I had ever heard said of the man whom an ironical fate has made master of the Old World.

Suddenly the manner of the Princess underwent a sudden change.

She rose to her feet and gave me a penetrating glance, a glance which revealed for the first time something of that commanding personality which had made this slight, exquisite creature for years one of the most able and successful of secret negotiators, and a person to be reckoned with by every foreign minister.

"You do not trust me, Andreas V— —. It is natural. You do not love me. It is possible that it is my fault. But I have sworn to save your life, and I will do it in your own despite. In order that I may succeed, I will forget that I am a woman, and I will forget that you regard me as a criminal. Come here! I will show you into my oratory, into which not even my confidential maid is ever allowed to penetrate. Perhaps what you will see there may convince you that I am neither a traitor nor a Delilah."

With the proud step of an empress, she led the way into the adjoining room, which was a bedroom sumptuously enriched with everything that could allure the senses. The very curtains of the bed seemed to breathe out languorous odors, the walls were hung with ravishing groups of figures that might have come from a Pompeiian temple, the dressing-table was rich with gold and gems.

Without pausing for an instant the mistress of the chamber walked straight across it to a narrow door let into the farther wall, and secured by a tiny lock like that of a safe.

Drawing a small key from her bosom, the Princess inserted it in the lock, leaving me to follow in a state of the most intense expectation.

The apartment in which I found myself was a narrow, white-washed cell like a prison, lit only by the flames of two tall wax candles which stood on a table, or rather an altar, at the far end.

Besides the altar, the sole object in the room was a wooden step in front of it. Over the altar, in accordance with the rule of the Greek Church, there hung a sacred picture. And below, between the two candlesticks, there rested two objects, the sight of which fairly took away my breath.

One was a photograph frame containing a portrait of myself—how obtained I shall never know. The portrait was framed with immortelles, the emblems of death, and the artist had given my face the ghastly pallor and rigidity of the face of a corpse.

The other object on the altar was a small whip of knotted leather thongs.

Without uttering a word, without even turning her head

to see if I had followed, the Princess Y—— knelt down on the step, stripped her shoulders with a singular determined gesture, and then, taking the knout in one hand, began to scourge the bare flesh.

Chapter 19 The Spirit of Madame Blavatsky

At the hour appointed by the Czar I presented myself at the Winter Palace to assist at the spiritualist experiments of M. Auguste.

I shall not attempt to describe the impression left by the weird scene in the Princess Y——'s oratory.

To those who do not know the Slav temperament, with its strange mixture of sensuality and devotion, of barbarous cruelty and over-civilized cunning, seldom far removed from the brink of insanity, the incident I have recorded will appear incredible. I have narrated it, simply because I have undertaken to narrate everything bearing on the business in which I was engaged. I am well aware that truth is stranger than fiction, and I should have little difficulty, if I were so disposed, in framing a story, full of plausible, commonplace incidents, which no one could doubt or dispute.

I have preferred to take a bolder course, knowing that although I may be discredited for a time, yet when historians in the future come to sift the secret records of the age, I shall be amply vindicated.

I shall only add that I did not linger a moment after the unhappy woman had begun her penance, if such it was, but withdrew from her presence and from the house without speaking a word.

The feelings with which I anticipated my encounter with the medium were very different. Whatever might be my doubts with regard to the unfortunate Sophia—and I honestly began to think that the suicide of Menken had affected her brain—I had no doubt whatever that M. Auguste was a thoroughly unscrupulous man.

The imperial servant to whom I was handed over at the entrance to the Czar's private apartments conducted me to what I imagine to have been the boudoir of the Czaritza, or at all events the family sitting room.

It was comfortably but plainly furnished in the English style, and was just such a room as one might find in the house of a London citizen, or a small country squire. I noticed that the wall-paper was faded, and the hearth-rug really worn out.

The Emperor of All the Russias was not alone. Seated beside him in front of the English grate was the beautiful young Empress, in whose society he finds a refuge from his greedy courtiers and often unscrupulous ministers, and who, I may add, has skilfully and successfully kept out of any entanglement in politics.

Rising at my entrance, Nicholas II. advanced and shook me by the hand.

"In this room," he told me, "there are no emperors and no empresses, only Mr. and Mrs. Nicholas."

He presented me to the Czaritza, who received me in the same style of simple friendliness, and then, pointing to a money-box which formed a conspicuous object on the mantel-shelf, he added:

"For every time the word 'majesty' is used in this room there is a fine of one ruble, which goes to our sick and wounded. So be careful, M. V— —."

In spite of this warning I did not fail to make a good many contributions to the money-box in the course of the evening. In my intercourse with royalty I model myself on the British Premier Beaconsfield, and I regard my rubles as well spent.

We all three spoke in English till the arrival of M. Auguste, who knew only French and a few words of Russian. I remarked afterward that the spirit of Madame Blavatsky, a Russian by birth, who had spent half her life in England, appeared to have lost the use of both languages in the other world, and communicated with us exclusively in French.

The appearance of M. Auguste did not help to overcome my prejudice against him. He had too evidently made up for the part of the mystic.

The hair of M. Auguste was black and long, his eyes rolled much in their sockets, and his costume was a compromise between the frock coat and the cassock.

But it was above all his manner that impressed me disagreeably. He affected to be continually falling into fits of abstraction, as if his communings with the spirits were diverting his attention from the affairs of earth. Even on his entrance he went through the forms of greeting his host and hostess as though scarcely conscious of their presence. I caught a sly look turned on myself, however, and when I was presented to him as "Mr. Sterling" his reception of the name made me think that he had expected something else.

The Czar having explained that I was a friend interested in spiritualism, in whose presence he wished to hear again from Madame Blavatsky, M. Auguste rolled his eyes formidably, and agreed to summon the departed theosophist.

A small round table was cleared of the Czaritza's work-basket—she had been knitting a soldier's comforter—and we took our seats around it. The electric light was switched off, so that we were in perfect darkness, except for the red glow of the coal fire.

A quarter of an hour or so passed in a solemn silence, broken only by occasional whispers from "Mr. Nicholas" or the medium.

"It is a long time answering," the Czar whispered at last.

"I fear there is a hostile influence," M. Auguste responded in the jargon of his craft.

Hardly had the words left his lips when a perfect shower of raps seemed to descend on all parts of the table at once.

Let me say here, once for all, that I am not prepared to offer any explanation of what happened on this occasion. I have read of some of the devices by which such illusions are produced, and I have no doubt a practised conjurer could have very easily fathomed the secrets of M. Auguste. But I had not come there with any intention of detecting or exposing him.

The medium pretended to address the author of the raps.

"If there is any hostile influence which prevents your communicating with us, rap twice."

Two tremendous raps nearly drowned the last word. The spirit seemed to be quick-tempered.

"If it is a woman, rap once——"

No response. This was decidedly clever.

"If it is myself, rap."

This time, instead of silence, there was a faint scratching under the surface of the table.

"The negative sign," M. Auguste explained blandly, for our benefit.

Then, addressing himself once more to the invisible member of the party, he inquired:

"If it is Mr. Nicholas, rap."

Silence.

"You must excuse me," the medium said, turning his face in my direction. "If it is Mr. Sterling— —"

A shower of raps. I really thought the table would have given way.

This was discouraging. The Czar came to my rescue, however.

"I particularly wish Mr. Sterling to be present," he observed with a touch of displeasure—whether intended for M. Auguste or the spiritual visitant I could not tell.

The hierophant no doubt saw that he must submit. His retreat was executed with great skill.

"If the obstacle is one that can be removed, rap once."

A rap.

"Can you spell it for us?"

In the rather cumbrous alphabet in use among the shades, the visitor spelled out in French:

"*Son nom.*"

"Is there something you object to about his name?"

A rap.

"Is it an assumed name?"

A very loud rap. Decidedly the spirit was indignant.

"Can you tell us his real name? His initials will do?"

"A. V." spelled the unseen visitor.

"Is that right?" M. Auguste inquired with well-assumed curiosity.

"It is marvelous!" ejaculated the Emperor. "You will understand, of course, Auguste, that this must be kept a secret among ourselves."

"Ask if it is Madame Blavatsky," said the Czar.

We learned that the apostle of theosophy was indeed present.

"Would you like to hear from any other spirits?" M. Auguste asked the company.

"I should be glad of a word with Bismarck," I suggested.

In five minutes the Iron Chancellor announced himself. His rap was sharp, quick and decided, quite a characteristic rap.

"Ask if he approves of the present policy of the German Emperor?"

A hearty rap. Evidently the spirit had greatly changed its views in the other world.

"Ask if he remembers telling me, the last time I saw him, that Russia was smothering Germany in bed?"

"Do you refuse to answer that question?" M. Auguste put in adroitly.

An expressive rap.

"Will you answer any other questions from this gentleman?"

Then the spirit of Bismarck spoke out. It denounced me as a worker of evil, a source of strife, and particularly as one who was acting injuriously to the Russian Empire. I confess M. Auguste scored.

"In his lifetime he would have said all that, if he had thought I was working in the interest of Russia and against Germany," I remarked in my own defence.

The spirit of the Iron Chancellor was dismissed, and that of Madame Blavatsky recalled.

It was evident that the Czar placed particular confidence in his late subject. Indeed, if the issues at stake had been less serious, I think I should have made an attempt to shake the

Emperor's blind faith in the performances of M. Auguste.

But my sole object was to read, if I could, the secret plans and intentions of a very different imperial character, whose agent I believed the spirit to be.

M. Auguste, I quickly discovered, was distracted between fear of offending Nicholas by too much reserve, and dread of enabling me to see his game. In the end the Czar's persistence triumphed, and we obtained something like a revelation.

"Tell us what you can see, that it concerns the Emperor to know," M. Auguste had adjured his familiar.

"I see"—the reply was rapped out with irritating slowness —I quite longed for a slate—"an English dockyard. The workmen are secretly at work by night, with muffled hammers. They are building a torpedo boat. It is to the order of the Japanese Government. The English police have received secret instructions from the Minister of the Interior not to interfere."

"Minister of the Interior" was a blunder. With my knowledge of English politics I am able to say that the correct title of this personage should be "Secretary of State for the Domestic Department." But few foreigners except myself have been able to master the intricacies of the British Constitution.

"For what is this torpedo boat designed?" M. Auguste inquired.

"It is for service against the Baltic Fleet. The Russian sailors are the bravest in the world, but they are too honest to be a match for the heathen Japanese," the spirit pursued, with some inconsistency.

I could not help reflecting that Madame Blavatsky in her lifetime had professed the Buddhist faith, which is that of the majority in Japan.

"Do you see anything else?"

"I see other dockyards where the same work is being carried on. A whole fleet of warships is being prepared by the perfidious British for use against the fleet of Russia."

"Ask her to cast her eye over the German dockyards," I put in.

"Spirits have no sex," M. Auguste corrected severely. "I will ask it."

A succession of raps conveyed the information that Germany was preserving a perfectly correct course, as usual. Her sole departure from the attitude of strict neutrality was to permit certain pilots, familiar with the North Sea navigation, to offer their services to the Russian fleet.

"Glance into the future," said the Czar. "Tell us what you see about to happen."

"I see the Baltic Fleet setting out. The Admiral has issued the strictest orders to neutral shipping to retire to their harbors and leave the sea clear for the warships of Russia. He has threatened to sink any neutral ship that comes within range of his guns.

"As long as he is in the Baltic these orders are obeyed. The German, Swedish and Danish flags are lowered at his approach, as is right.

"Now he passes out into the North Sea. The haughty and hostile English defy his commands. Their merchant ships go forth as usual. Presuming on their knowledge of international law, they annoy and vex the Russian warships by sailing past them. The blood of the brave Russian officers begins to boil. Ask me no more."

M. Auguste, prompted by the deeply interested Czar, did

ask more.

"I see," the obedient seeress resumed, "torpedo boats secretly creeping out from the British ports. They do not openly fly the Japanese flag, but lurk among the English ships, with the connivance of the treacherous islanders.

"The Baltic Fleet approaches. The torpedo boats, skulking behind the shelter of their friends, steal closer to the Russian ships. Then the brave Russian Admiral remembers his promise. Just in time to save his fleet from destruction, he signals to the British to retire.

"They obstinately refuse. The Russian fleet opens fire.

"I can see no more."

The spirit of the seeress, it will be observed, broke off its revelations at the most interesting point, with the skill of a practised writer of serials.

But the Czar, fairly carried away by excitement, insisted on knowing more.

"Ask the spirit if there will be any foreign complications," he said.

I had already remarked that our invisible companion showed a good deal of deference to the wishes of Nicholas II., perhaps in his character of Head of the Orthodox Church.

After a little hesitation it rapped out:

"The English are angry, but they are restrained by the fear of Germany. The German Michael casts his shield in front of Russia, and the islanders are cowed. I cannot see all that follows. But in the end I see that the Yellow Peril is averted by the joint action of Russia and Germany."

This answer confirmed to the full my suspicions regarding the source of M. Auguste's inspiration. I believed firmly that there was a spirit present, but it was not the spirit of the deceased theosophist, rather of a monarch who is very much alive.

The medium now professed to feel exhausted, and Madame Blavatsky was permitted to retire.

I rose to accompany M. Auguste as soon as he made a move to retire.

"If you will let me drive you as far as my hotel," I said to him, "I think I can show you something which will repay you for coming with me."

The wizard looked me in the face for the first time, as he said deliberately:

"I shall be very pleased to come."

I said as little as possible during the drive homeward.

My companion was equally silent. No doubt he, like myself, was bracing himself for a duel of wits.

As soon as we were safe in my private room at the hotel, with a bottle of vodka and a box of cigars in front of us, I opened the discussion with my habitual directness.

"I need not tell you, M. Auguste, that I have not invited you here to discuss questions of psychology. I am a politician, and it matters nothing to me whether I am dealing with a ghost or a man, provided I can make myself understood."

M. Auguste bowed.

"For instance, it is quite clear that the interesting revelations we have had to-night would not have been made without your good will. It is to be presumed, therefore, that if I can convince you that it is better to turn the Emperor's mind in another direction, you will refuse to make yourself the medium of further communications of that precise character."

M. Auguste gave me an intelligent glance.

"I am as you have just said, a *medium*," he replied with significant emphasis. "As such, I need not tell you, I have no personal interest in the communications which are made through me."

I nodded, and took out my pocket-book, from which I extracted a hundred ruble-note (about $75).

"I promised to show you something interesting," I remarked, as I laid it on the table.

M. Auguste turned his head, and his lip curled slightly.

"I am afraid my sight is not very good," he said

negligently. "Is not that object rather small?"

"It is merely a specimen," I responded, counting out nine others, and laying them beside the first.

"Ah, now I fancy I can see what you are showing me," he admitted.

"There is a history attached to these notes," I explained. "They represent the amount of a bet which I have just won."

"Really! That is most interesting."

"I now have another bet of similar nature pending, which I hope also to be able to win."

"I am tempted to wish you success," put in the medium encouragingly.

"The chances of success are so great that if you were a betting man I should be inclined to ask you to make a joint affair of it," I said.

"My dear M. V——, I am not a bigot. I have no objection to a wager provided the stakes are made worth my while."

"I think they should be. Well, I will tell you plainly, I stand to win this amount if the Baltic Fleet does not sail for another month."

M. Auguste smiled pleasantly.

"I congratulate you," he said. "From what I have heard the repairs will take at least that time."

"But that is not all. This bet of mine is continuous. I win a similar stake for every month which passes without the fleet having left harbor."

M. Auguste gazed at me steadily before speaking.

"If your bet were renewable weekly instead of monthly, you might become quite a rich man."

I saw that I was dealing with a cormorant. I made a hasty

mental calculation. Half of one thousand rubles was about $375 a week, and the information I had led me to believe that Port Arthur was capable of holding out for another six months at least. To delay the sailing of the Baltic Fleet till then would cost roughly $10,000—say 15,000 rubles.

I decided that neither England nor Japan would grudge the price.

"I think your suggestion is a good one," I answered M. Auguste. "In that case, should you be willing to share the bet?"

"I should be willing to undertake it entirely," was the response.

The scoundrel wanted $20,000!

Had I been dealing with an honest man I should have let him have the money. But he had raised his terms so artfully that I felt sure that if I yielded this he would at once make some fresh demand.

I therefore shook my head, and began picking up the notes on the table.

"That would not suit me at all," I said decidedly. "I do not wish to be left out altogether."

M. Auguste watched me with growing uneasiness as I restored the notes one by one to my pocket-book.

"Look here!" he said abruptly, as the last note disappeared. "Tell me plainly what you expect me to do."

"I expect you to have a communication from your friend Madame Blavatsky, or any other spirit you may prefer—Peter the Great would be most effective, I should think—every time the Baltic Fleet is ready to start, warning 'Mr. Nicholas' not to let it sail."

M. Auguste appeared to turn this proposal over in his

mind.

"And is that all?" he asked.

"I shall expect you to keep perfect secrecy about the arrangement. I have a friend at Potsdam, and I shall be pretty sure to hear if you try to give me away."

"Potsdam!" M. Auguste seemed genuinely surprised, and even disconcerted.

"Do you mean to say that you didn't know you were carrying out the instructions of Wilhelm II.?" I demanded, scarcely less surprised.

It was difficult to believe that the vexation showed by the medium was feigned.

"Of course! I see it now!" burst from him. "I wondered what she meant by all that stuff about Germany. And I—a Frenchman!"

It is extraordinary what unexpected scruples will display themselves in the most unprincipled knaves. Low as they may descend, there seems always to be some one point on which they are as sensitive as a Bayard.

M. Auguste, of all men in the world, was a French patriot! It turned out that he was a fanatical Nationalist and anti-Semite. He had howled in anti-Dreyfusite mobs, and flung stones at the windows of Masonic temples in Paris.

I was delighted with this discovery, which gave me a stronger hold on him than any bribe could.

But I had noted the feminine pronoun in his exclamation recorded above. I did not think it referred to the revealing spirit.

"You have been deceived by the woman who has given you your instructions," I remarked to him, when his excitement had subsided a little. "I fancy I can guess her name."

"Yes. It is the Princess Y— —," he confessed.

Bewildering personality! Again, as I heard her name connected with an intrigue of the basest kind, a criminal conspiracy to influence the ruler of Russia by feigned revelations from the spirits of the dead, I recalled the sight I had last had of her, kneeling in her oratory, scourging herself before—my portrait!

There was no longer any fear that M. Auguste would prove obdurate on the question of terms. He pocketed his first five hundred rubles, and departed, vowing that the Baltic fleet should never get farther than Libau, if it was in the power of spirits to prevent it.

Desirous to relieve Lord Bedale's mind as far as possible I despatched the following wire to him the next morning:

Sailing of Baltic Fleet postponed indefinitely. No danger for the present. Watch Germany.

I sent a fuller account of the situation to a son of Mr. Katahashi, who was in England, nominally attached to the staff of the Imperial Bank, but really on business of a confidential character which it would be indiscreet on my part to indicate.

I may say that I particularly cautioned the young Japanese to avoid any action calculated to give the least color to the German legends about warships being secretly manufactured in British yards to the order of the Mikado's Government.

Every reader who has followed the course of the war with any attention will recollect the history of the fleet thus detained by my contrivance.

Week after week, and month after month, the Baltic Fleet was declared to be on the point of departure. Time after time the Czar went on board to review it in person, and speak words of encouragement to the officers and crew. And every time, after everything had been pronounced ready, some mysterious obstacle arose at the last moment to detain the fleet in Russian waters.

Journalists, naval experts, politicians and other ill-informed persons invented or repeated all sorts of explanations to account for the series of delays.

Only in the very innermost circles of the Russian Court it was whispered that the guardian spirit of the great Peter, the founder of Russia's naval power, had repeatedly come to warn his descendant of disasters in store for the fleet, should it be permitted to sail.

M. Auguste was earning his reward.

Chapter 21 The Funeral

The extreme privacy with which I had managed my negotiation with M. Auguste completely baffled the plotters who were relying on the voyage of the Baltic Fleet to furnish a *casus belli* between Russia and Great Britain.

They realized, of course, that some powerful hand was interfering with their designs, and they were sufficiently intelligent to guess that that hand must be mine.

But they were far from suspecting the method of my operations. They firmly believed that M. Auguste was still carrying out their instructions, and sowing distrust of England in the mind of Nicholas II. Indeed, on one occasion he informed me that the Princess Y— — had sent for him and ordered him not to frighten the Czar to such an extent as to make him afraid to let the fleet proceed to sea.

Unable to detect and countermine me, it was natural that they should become impatient for my removal.

Accordingly, I was not surprised to receive an urgent message from Sophia, late one evening, requesting me to come to her without delay.

By this time our friendship, if such it could be called, had become so intimate that I visited her nearly every day on one pretext or another.

Her greeting, as soon as I had obeyed the summons, showed me that a fresh development had taken place in the situation.

"Andreas, the hour has come!"

"The hour?"

"For your removal. Petrovitch has been here. He suspects

something. He has rebuked me severely for the delay."

"Did you tell him I was not an easy man to kill?"

"I told him anything and everything. He would not listen. He says they have lost confidence in me. He was brutal. He said — —"

"Well, what did he say?"

"He said—" she spoke slowly and shamefacedly—"that he perceived it took a man to kill a man."

I smiled grimly.

"History tells us differently. But what then?"

"To-morrow I shall no longer be able to answer for your life."

"You think some one else will be appointed to dispose of me?"

"I am sure that some one else has been appointed already. Most likely it is Petrovitch himself."

"Well, I shall look out for him." I did not think it necessary to tell Sophia that I had been expecting something of this kind, and had made certain preparations.

"It will be useless, Andreas. You do not know the man with whom you have to deal."

"The ignorance may be mutual," I observed drily.

The Princess became violently agitated.

"You must let me save you," she exclaimed clasping her hands.

"In what way?"

"You must let me kill you *here*, to-night.

"Don't you understand?" she pursued breathlessly. "It is absolutely necessary for your safety, perhaps for the safety of both of us, that they should think I have carried out my instructions. You must appear to die. Then they will no longer concern themselves about you, and you will be able to assume some other personality without being suspected."

The scheme appealed to me strongly, all the more that it seemed as though it could be made to fit in very well with my own plans.

"You are a clever woman, Sophia," I said cautiously. "How do you purpose to carry out your scheme? They will want to see my corpse, I suppose."

She drew out the little key I have already described.

"Come this way."

I followed her through the bedroom as before to the door of the locked oratory.

She opened the door and admitted me.

By the light of the wax candles I saw what was surely one of the strangest sights ever presented to mortal eyes.

It was myself, lying in state!

On a high bier draped in white and black cloth, I lay, or, rather, my counterpart presentment in wax lay, wrapped and shrouded like a dead body, a branch of palm in the closed hands, and a small Russian coin resting on the lips, in accordance with a quaint custom which formerly prevailed in many lands.

In spite of my habitual self-command I was unable to repress a cold shiver at this truly appalling spectacle.

"Your stage management is perfect," I observed after a pause. "But will they be satisfied with a look only?"

"I do not think so. It will be necessary for you to put on the appearance of death for a short time, till I have satisfied them. Afterward I can conceal you in here, while this—" she pointed to the ghastly figure—"is buried under your name."

"Let us get back to the other room, before we talk about it," I urged. "This is not altogether a pleasant sight."

As we passed out of the oratory I stealthily took note of the fastening of the door. The lock was on the outside only; in other words, if I permitted myself to be immured in the cell-like chamber, I should be a prisoner at the mercy of my charming friend.

"And now, by what means do you purpose that I shall assume the appearance of death?" I inquired as soon as we had returned to the boudoir.

The Princess opened a small cabinet, and produced a tiny stoppered bottle.

"By swallowing this medicine," she answered. "I have had it specially prepared from a recipe given me ten years ago at a time when I thought of resorting to the same contrivance to escape from my taskmaster."

I took the bottle in my hand, and examined it carefully. It bore no label, and the contents appeared perfectly colorless.

"In five minutes after you have swallowed the contents of the bottle," Sophia explained, "you will begin to turn cold, at first in the feet and hands. As the cold mounts to the brain you will gradually lose consciousness, and become rigid. You will look as pale as if you were actually dead, and your heart will cease to beat."

"And how long will this stupor last?"

"About twenty-four hours, more or less, according to your constitution."

I looked carefully and steadily into her eyes. She flushed and trembled violently, but did not quail.

"What does it taste like?" I asked.

"It is a little bitter."

"I will take it in water, then."

"You can take it in wine, if you like. I have some here."

She moved to a small cupboard in the wall.

"I shall tell them that I gave it to you in wine, in any case," she added.

"I prefer water, thank you. May I fetch some from the next room?"

"I will fetch it," she said hastily, going to the bedroom.

On an ebony stand beside me there was a large china bowl containing a flowering plant in its pot. In a second I had removed the stopper, emptied the bottle into the space between the flower-pot and the outer bowl, and put the stopper back again.

"Tell me," I said to the Princess as she hurried back with a carafe and tumbler, "have you thought how I am to get away from this house without exciting attention?"

"It will be easy for me to procure you a dozen disguises. I am always going to masked balls. But are you in such a hurry to leave me?"

"I shall find the air of your oratory rather confined, I am afraid."

She hung her head in evident chagrin.

"But where will you go?" she demanded.

"Oh, that is all arranged. I have taken a small house and furnished it, in another name."

"Where?" she asked breathlessly.

"Perhaps I had better not tell you till this excitement is over. I must not burden you with too many of my secrets."

Sophia's eyes filled with tears.

"You distrust me still!" she cried. "But, after all, what does it matter? I have only to ask Petrovitch."

"That will be quite unnecessary as well as useless. I pledge myself to tell you before I leave this place, and I have not favored M. Petrovitch with my new address."

She smiled scornfully.

"And do you believe that you have succeeded in taking a house in Petersburg without his knowledge? You do not know him, I tell you again. He has had you watched every hour of the day while you have been here."

"Please credit me with a little resource, as well as your friend," I answered with some slight irritation. "I have no doubt the spies of M. Petrovitch have watched me pretty closely, but they have not been able to watch every person who has come in and out of the hotel. Two of my most capable assistants have been in Petersburg for the last month—since the day you hinted that my life was not quite safe, in fact."

The woman before me looked completely overwhelmed.

"One of them," I proceeded with cutting severity, "has taken the house I speak of. The other is watching over my personal safety at this moment."

The Princess fairly gave way. Sinking on the couch behind her, she exclaimed in a faint voice:

"You are a demon, not a man!"

It was the finest compliment she could have paid me.

"And now," I said carelessly, "to carry out your admirable little idea."

The unhappy woman put up her hands, and turned away her head in sheer terror.

I splashed some water into the tumbler, and then trickled

in a small quantity afterward, to imitate the sound of adding the poison. This done I respectfully handed the bottle to my companion.

"To our next meeting!" I called out lightly, as I lifted the tumbler to my lips and drained it.

It was the Princess who swooned.

Although I had not foreseen this weakness on her part I took advantage of it to draw the tiny key of the oratory from her bosom, and hide it in my mouth.

I then touched the bell twice, the signal for the Princess's maid to appear.

"Fauchette," I said, when she entered—for this was the assistant I had alluded to as watching over my personal safety —"Madame has just given me the contents of that stoppered bottle. Do you know anything about them?"

Fauchette had made good use of her time since obtaining her situation. These things are so easily managed that I am almost ashamed to explain that a bribe to the former maid had brought about a convenient illness, and the recommendation of Fauchette as a temporary substitute.

"Yes, Monsieur," she said quietly. "I filled the bottle with water this afternoon, in case of accident. I have preserved the previous contents, in case you should care to have them analyzed."

"You have done well, very well, my girl."

Fauchette blushed with pleasure. I do not often say so much to my staff.

"Madame does not know that I had just emptied the bottle into that china bowl," I added carelessly.

"It is useless to try to serve Monsieur; he does everything

himself," murmured the poor girl, mortified.

"Nonsense, Fauchette, I have just praised you. It is always possible that I may overlook something."

Fauchette shook her head with an incredulous air.

I have found it good policy to maintain this character for infallibility with my staff. It is true, perhaps, that I do not very often blunder.

"And now," I went on, "it is time for the poison to take effect! As soon as I am dead, you will awake Madame."

I lay down on another couch, and composed myself in a rigid attitude with my eyes closed. I did not believe, of course, that it would be possible to deceive a close observer, but I trusted to the wild emotions of the Princess to blind her to any signs of life.

I heard Fauchette dart on her mistress with a well-acted scream, and sprinkle her face and neck with cold water.

Sophia seemed to revive quickly.

"Andreas!" I heard her gasp. "Where? What has become of him?"

"M. Sterling has also fainted," the maid replied with assumed innocence.

"Ha!"

It was more like a shriek than a sob. I heard a hasty rustling of skirts, and then Sophia seemed to be kneeling beside me, and feeling for the beat of my heart.

"Go, Fauchette! Send Gregory instantly to M. Petrovitch to inform him that M. Sterling has been taken ill in my house, and that I fear he is dead."

The Princess began loosening my necktie.

Had Fauchette been present I should have been able to

point to this as a proof that I was not incapable of an occasional oversight.

As a matter of fact, I had not anticipated this very natural action on Sophia's part. Yet it should have been evident that, were it only to keep up appearances before any one who might come to view my supposed corpse, she would be bound to free my neck.

And I was wearing the locket which contained the portrait of my promised bride!

I lay, really rigid with apprehension, while Sophia's caressing fingers tenderly removed the necktie, and began unfastening my collar and shirt.

Suddenly I heard an ejaculation—at first striking the note of surprise and curiosity merely, but deepening to fear.

In a moment the locket was lifted from my chest, and forced open with a metallic click.

"Ah!—Ah!"

She let the open locket drop from her fingers on my bare throat.

Instantly it was clutched up again. I could picture the frenzied gaze of jealousy and hate in those burning eyes of deepest violet; I could actually feel the passionate breathing from between the clenched teeth of whitest ivory.

"Miserable child!" she hissed, the hand that held the locket trembling so that I could feel it against my neck. "So *you* have robbed me of him!"

She paused, and then added, forcing out each word with a passion of distilled hate——

"But you shall never have him! He shall be mine! Mine! Mine, in the grave!"

Chapter 22 A Perilous Moment

I lay with every nerve strained to its utmost tension, listening for the least movement on the part of the maddened woman which might indicate she was about to stab me then and there.

In the silence that followed, if she did not hear the beating of my heart it was only because her own stormy emotions had rendered her deaf and blind to everything else.

For a time her rapid breathing continued to warm my uncovered neck. Then she snapped-to the locket and let it fall, and rose from my side to pace the floor of the room with swift, irregular steps.

Fauchette, who must have been anxious to know how I was faring, now came back without waiting to be summoned.

"Well?" the Princess demanded, halting in her promenade.

"Gregory has gone for M. Petrovitch, Madame. Is there anything I can do?"

"I have tried every restorative," came the answer. "See if you can detect any signs of life."

The last command seemed to come as an afterthought. No doubt, Sophia wished to test her work before Petrovitch arrived.

I was encouraged to think that she had no immediate intention of killing me; and as the maid bent over me I contrived to give her hand a reassuring squeeze.

"He is quite dead, Madame," the girl said, turning away. "Would you like to have the body carried into another room?"

"No. Wait till M. Petrovitch comes," her mistress replied. "You can go."

As my assistant withdrew I again became on the alert for any dangerous move on the part of the Princess.

It was not long before I was conscious that the room had grown darker.

I gathered that Sophia had switched off some of the lights in order to make it more difficult for Petrovitch to detect her fraud, and again I took courage.

Some muttered words helped me to understand the plan of the desperate woman.

"I will give him one chance. He shall choose. Men do not die for love in these days."

There was little doubt that she intended to lock me up in her oratory and hold me a prisoner till I consented to sacrifice my faith to her Japanese rival.

Satisfied that there was little risk of any immediate violence, I waited calmly for the arrival of Sophia's colleague, or master.

The head of the Manchurian Syndicate lost no time on the way. Very soon I heard the door open and the familiar voice, with its slightly affected accent, saying,

"Permit me to offer you the expression of my sincere regrets, dear Princess! — And my sincere congratulations," he added in a more business-like tone, as the door closed again.

A sigh was the only audible response.

"It has cost you something, I can see," the man's voice resumed soothingly. "That fact gives you a still stronger claim on our gratitude. I confess I began to fear seriously that you were deceiving us, and that would have been very dangerous."

Another obscure sound, between a sigh and a sob, from the woman.

"Now we can proceed with light hearts. Within three months from now Russia and Great Britain will be at war. I do not mind answering for it. There was only one man in Europe who could have prevented it, and he lies there!"

"You would have it so! I still say it would have been enough to imprison him somewhere."

"You talk foolishly, believe me, Princess. A man like that is not to be imprisoned. There is no jailer in the world who would venture to undertake to keep the famous A. V. under lock and key."

"I would have undertaken it," came the answer. "I would have locked him in my oratory, the key of which never leaves my bosom."

"Nevertheless if it was important to that man to steal it from you, it would not remain in your bosom very long."

A startled cry interrupted the speaker, and told me that Sophia had made the fatal discovery of the loss of her key.

I held my breath in the most dreadful suspense. Everything now depended on this woman. If she allowed the least hint, I knew that Petrovitch would never leave the room without at least an attempt to change my supposed trance into death.

Fortunately the Princess was equal to the emergency. I heard her give a slight laugh.

"I am punished for my assurance," she confessed. "I am not quite hardened, as you know; and when I realized that M. V —— was actually dead, I was obliged to pray for him. I have left the key in the door."

"Go and fetch it, then."

The tone in which these words were spoken was harsh. I

heard Sophia going out of the room, and in an instant, with a single bound, as it seemed, the man was leaning over me, feeling my pulse, listening for my heart, and testing whether I breathed.

"If I had brought so much as a knife with me, I would have made sure," I heard him mutter to himself.

Fortunately Sophia's absence did not last ten seconds. She must have snatched up the first key that came to hand, that of a jewel-box most likely, and hurried back with it.

Petrovitch seemed to turn away from me with reluctance.

"You doubt me, it appears," came in angry tones from the Princess.

"I doubt everybody," was the cool rejoinder. "You were in love with this fellow."

"You think so? Then look at this."

I felt the locket being picked up, and heard the click of the tiny spring.

A coarse laugh burst from the financier.

"So that is it! Woman's jealousy is safer than her sworn word, after all. Now I believe he *is* dead."

The Princess made no reply.

Presently the man spoke again.

"This must be kept a secret among ourselves, you understand. The truth is, I have exceeded my instructions a little. A certain personage only authorized detention. It appears he is like you in having a certain tenderness for this fellow—why, I can't think. At any rate his manner was rather alarming when we hinted that a coffin made the safest straight-jacket."

It was impossible for me to doubt that it was the Kaiser whom this villain had insulted by offering to have me assassinated. I thanked Wilhelm II. silently for his chivalrous behavior. M. Petrovitch could have known little of the proud Hohenzollern whom he tempted.

At the same time, it was a source of serious concern for me to know that, just as I had learned that my real opponent was my friend the Kaiser, so he in turn had acquired the knowledge that he had me against him.

It had become a struggle, no longer in the dark, between the most resourceful of Continental sovereigns and myself, and that being so, I realized that I could not afford to rest long on my oars.

From the deep breathing of the Princess, I surmised that she was choking down the rage she must have felt at the other's cynical depravity. For Sophia, though capable of committing a murder out of jealousy perhaps, was yet incapable of killing for reward.

"Well," I heard Petrovitch say in the tone of one who is taking his leave, "I must send some one 'round to remove our friend."

"Do not trouble, if you please. I will see to the funeral," came in icy tones from the Princess.

"What, still sentimental! Be careful, my good Sophia Y — —, you will lose your value to us if you give way to such weaknesses."

I heard his steps move across the carpeted floor, and then with startling suddenness, the words came out:

"Curse me if I can believe he *is* dead!"

My blood ran cold. But it turned out to be only a passing exclamation. At the end of what seemed to me minutes—they can only have been seconds—the footsteps moved on, and the door opened and closed.

"Thank God!" burst from Sophia.

Her next words were plainly an apostrophe to myself.

"So you did not trust me after all!"

I was within an ace of opening my eyes on the supposition that she had found me out, when I was reassured by her adding, this time to herself,

"He must have done it when I fainted!"

I saw that she was referring to my theft of the key.

There was a soft rustle of silk on the floor, and I felt her hands searching in my pockets for the stolen key.

"Fool! To think that I could outwit him!" she murmured to herself at last.

She had taken some time to learn the lesson, however.

It was soon evident that the Princess Y— — had taken her new maid into her confidence to a certain extent.

She must have rung for Fauchette without my hearing anything, for presently the door opened again, and I heard my assistant's voice.

As the result of a hurried consultation between the two women, in which Fauchette played to perfection the part of a devoted maid who is only desirous to anticipate the wishes of her mistress, it was decided to wheel the sofa on which I lay into the oratory, and to bring the wax dummy into the Princess's bedroom, to lie in state till the next day.

The arrangement did not take long to carry out.

Partly from what I was able to overhear, and partly from the report afterward furnished to me by Fauchette, I am able to relate succinctly what took place.

To begin with, I was left in the oratory, while the counterfeit corpse was duly arranged in the adjoining room.

Unable to lock me in the smaller apartment, Sophia declared her intention of locking both the outer doors of the bedroom, one of which gave on a corridor, while the other, as the reader is aware, opened into the boudoir where the previous scene had taken place.

The Princess retained one of these keys herself, entrusting the other to the maid, of course with the strictest injunctions as to its use.

To keep up appearances before the household, the Princess arranged to pass the next few nights in another room on the same floor, which usually served as a guest chamber.

It was explained to the servants that the death which had occurred had upset the nerves of their mistress, and rendered her own suite of rooms distasteful to her for the present.

Fauchette, who thus became my jailer, brought me a supply of cold food and wine during the night. I had part of this provision under the altar of the oratory, to serve me during the following day.

My cataleptic condition was supposed to endure for nearly twenty-four hours. The enforced seclusion was intensely irritating to a man of my temperament; but I could not evade it without revealing to Sophia that I had heard her confession, and thereby inflicting a deadly wound on a woman who loved me.

Meanwhile the arrangements for my funeral had been pressed on.

Already a telegram had appeared in the London papers announcing the sudden and unexpected death from heart-failure of the well-known English philanthropist, Mr. Melchisedak Sterling. One or two of the journals commented on the fact of Mr. Sterling's death having taken place while he was on a mission of peace to the Russian capital, and expressed a hope that his death would have a chastening effect on the War Party in Petersburg.

My friend, the editor of the Peace Review, very generously sent a wreath, which arrived too late for the funeral but was laid on my grave.

Unfortunately these newspaper announcements were taken seriously by my exalted employers, as well as by the enemies whom I wished to deceive, but this could not be helped.

By noon the undertaker's men had arrived with my coffin. The Princess played upon their ignorance of English customs and burial rites to pretend that the work of coffining must be done by women's hands. In this way she and Fauchette were able to enclose the dummy in its wooden shell, leaving to the men only the task of screwing down the lid.

The burial took place in the English cemetery. I am glad to say that the Princess contrived to avoid the mockery of a religious service by alleging that Mr. Sterling had belonged to a peculiar sect—the Quakers, I fancy—which holds such ceremonies to be worldly and unnecessary.

I may add that I have since visited my grave, which is still to be seen in a corner of the cemetery. It is marked by a stone slab with an inscription in English.

In the afternoon the faithful Fauchette persuaded her mistress to go out for a drive, to soothe her over-strained nerves.

Before quitting the house, the Princess came in to take a last look at me.

She lingered minute after minute, as though with some premonition that our next meeting would be under widely different circumstances.

To herself, I heard her whisper, sighing softly:

"Andreas! O Andreas! If I could sleep, or thou couldst never wake!"

She crept away, and the better to secure me locked both the bedroom doors herself, and carried off the keys.

On her return, two hours later, Sophia, with a look that told the watchful Fauchette of her uneasiness, hurried straight up-stairs, toward the door of the little oratory.

She found it locked from the outside, with the key in the door.

It had cost me something to break my pledge to the

Princess Y— — that I would give her my new address before leaving her.

But her unfortunate discovery of the portrait I wore around my neck and her plainly-declared intention to hold me a prisoner till she could shake my fidelity, had rendered it necessary for me to meet treachery with treachery.

The secret service, it must always be borne in mind, has its own code of honor, differing on many points from that obtaining in other careers, but perhaps stricter on the whole.

For instance, I can lay my hand on my heart and declare that I have never done either of two things which are done every day by men holding high offices and high places in the world's esteem. I have never taken a secret commission. And I have never taken advantage of my political information to gamble in stocks.

The manner of my escape was simplicity itself.

My assistant had not come to live with the Princess without making some preparations for the part she was to play, and these included the bringing with her of a bunch of skeleton keys, fully equal to the work of opening any ordinary lock.

As soon as her mistress was safely out of the way, Fauchette came to receive my instructions.

I told her that I did not intend to wait for my jailer's return. We discussed the best way for me to slip out, without obstruction from the servants, and I decided to take advantage of the superstition of the Russian illiterate class, by enacting the part of my own ghost.

The report that I had been buried without any funeral service had already reached the household, and had prepared them for any supernatural manifestation.

Fauchette first brought me a little powdered chalk, with

which I smeared my face. I then put on a long flowing cloak and a sombrero hat, part of the wardrobe accumulated by the Princess in the course of her gaieties.

I slipped a damp sponge into my pocket and directed the girl to lead the way.

She went down-stairs a few yards in front of me, turned into the servants' part of the house and threw open the back door, which led out into a courtyard giving on a street used only by tradesmen's carts. At this hour of the day it was deserted.

I followed cautiously in Fauchette's wake, and got as far as the back door without meeting any interruption.

But at that point, the porter, who must have been roused by an unfamiliar step—though I understand he swore afterward that the passage of the ghost had been absolutely noiseless— came out and stood in the doorway.

Without hesitating for an instant I assumed an erect posture and advanced swiftly toward him with my whitened face well displayed.

The fellow gave vent to a half-articulate call which died down in his throat, and bolted back into his room uttering yell after yell.

Fifteen seconds later I was out in the street, sponging the chalk from my face.

And five minutes after that I was comfortably seated in a hired droshky, on my way to a certain little house in the seafaring quarter of the city, which possessed, among other advantages, that of commanding an exceedingly fine view of the Admiralty Pier.

Chapter 24 A Secret Execution

I now come to a part of my chronicle which I plainly foresee must expose me to grave criticism.

To that criticism it is no part of my purpose to attempt any reply.

In the long run, I have found, men's minds are not much affected by argument and advocacy. Facts tell their own story, and men's judgments are usually the result of their personal prejudices.

For that reason I shall confine myself to relating facts. I have already told the story of my murder—for such it was in the intent—by Petrovitch. I shall now tell the story of the justice meted out by me on the assassin.

As soon as I was safely lodged in my house on the Alexander Quay, I despatched my assistant, a clever young Frenchman named Breuil, with a message to the promoter of the Manchurian Syndicate—the real moving spirit of that War clique in which even the bellicose grand dukes had only secondary parts.

The wording of the message had been carefully calculated to arouse curiosity, but not apprehension.

"The agent of a foreign Power," Breuil was instructed to say to this self-styled patriot, "with very large funds at his disposal, desires to see you in strict secrecy."

The bait took. Petrovitch, naturally concluding that he was to be offered a heavy bribe for some act of treachery to Russia, greedily accepted the invitation.

The infatuated man did not take even the ordinary precaution of asking for guarantees. He consented to accompany

Breuil at once, merely asking how far he had to go. This recklessness was the result of his supposed triumphant crime. Believing that I was safely interred in the English cemetery, he thought there was no one left for him to fear.

On the way he did his best to extract some information out of my assistant. But Breuil returned the same answer to all his questions and hints:

"I am under orders not to converse with you, monsieur."

The doomed man was in good spirits as the droshky put him down at the door of my house.

"Decidedly an out-of-the-way retreat!" he commented gaily. "I should hardly be able to find my way here again without your assistance!"

The silent Breuil merely bowed, as he proceeded to open the street door with a latch key.

Perhaps Petrovitch had been a little more nervous than he allowed to appear. When he noticed that his escort simply closed the door on the latch, without locking or bolting it further, he said in a tone of relief:

"You are not much afraid of being visited by the police, I see."

Breuil, as silent as ever, led the way into a back parlor, overlooking the Neva, where I was waiting to receive my visitor.

The room was plainly furnished as a study, and I had placed myself in an arm-chair facing the window, so that my back was turned to the door as Petrovitch entered.

I pretended to be writing furiously, as a pretext for not turning my head till the visitor had seated himself.

Breuil said quietly, "M. Petrovitch is here," and went out of the room.

As the door closed I tossed away my pen and turned around, facing my assassin.

"I am pleased to see you, M. Petrovitch."

"Monsieur V— —!"

I thought he would have lost his senses. His whole countenance changed. He clung to his chair, and his eyes were fixed on me with an expression of panic.

So complete was his collapse that he did not attempt to speak or excuse himself. I saw that he was hardly in a condition to listen to anything I had to say.

"I fear you are unwell, M. Petrovitch. Allow me to offer you a little brandy."

The wretched man watched me with bewildered looks, as I took a bottle and glasses from a cupboard and helped first him and then myself.

"It is quite wholesome, I assure you."

As I said the words I raised my own glass to my lips and sipped.

A choking cry escaped from the author of the war. He seized the glass I had set before him and feverishly drained it.

I saw that he was burning to know by what means I had escaped the fate prepared for me. But I had no object in gratifying his curiosity, and mere boasting is not a weakness of mine.

Steadfastly preserving the tone of a business interview between men who understand each other, I went on to say:

"I am here, as you know, in the joint interests of England and Japan."

My murderer nodded faintly. I could see him making a tremendous effort to control his nerves, and enter into conversation with me on my own terms.

"I think I should be glad of a little more brandy. Thank you!—I am not at all myself."

I shook my head compassionately.

"You should be careful to avoid too much excitement," I said. "Any sudden shock is bad for a man with your nerves."

The promoter gasped. The situation was clearly beyond him.

"You," I went on in my most matter-of-fact tone, "on the contrary, are acting on behalf of Germany."

"Who says so!" He was beginning to speak fiercely; but his eye met mine, and the words died on his lips.

"We will say I dreamed it, if you like," I responded drily. "I have very remarkable dreams sometimes, and learn a great deal from them.

"To confine ourselves to business. I have caused the sailing of this Baltic Fleet to be put off, because——"

"You—have caused it!"

The interruption burst from him in spite of himself.

I affected to shrug my shoulders with a certain annoyance.

"Your opinion of my powers does not seem to be a very high one, unfortunately," I remarked with irony. "It would be better if you accepted me as a serious antagonist, believe me."

Petrovitch lowered his eyes in confusion, as he muttered,

"I apologize, Monsieur V——. I have blundered, as I now perceive."

"Let us resume. I was about to say that I had prevented the sailing of this fleet, because I feared that its voyage might be marked by some incident likely to bring Great Britain and

Russia into collision."

The financier raised his head and watched me keenly.

"You, yourself, M. Petrovitch, have been active, I believe, in preparing the mind of the Czar and the Russian public for something of the sort. Doubtless you have not done so without very good grounds."

"My information leads me to think that a flotilla of torpedo boats is being kept ready in the English ports for a night attack on our fleet during its progress through the North Sea."

I smiled disdainfully.

"That is a false report. I have asked you to call here in the hope that I might find you ready to assist me in discrediting it."

The Russian continued to watch me out of his narrow eyes.

"And, also," I added, "to assist me in preventing any attempt to give color to it."

"I am not sure that I understand you, Monsieur V— —."

"That is quite possible. I will speak more plainly. There are some prophets who take a little trouble to make their prophesies come true. I wish to know whether you and your friends have determined that this particular prophesy shall come true—perhaps to fulfill it yourselves?"

Petrovitch frowned and compressed his lips.

"So that is why you got me here?"

"I wished to see," I said blandly, "if it was possible for me to offer you terms which might induce you to alter your views altogether—in short, to stop the war."

The financier looked thunderstruck.

"Monsieur V— —, you don't know what you ask! But you—would a million rubles tempt you to come over, to be neutral, even?"

"I am a member, by adoption, of the imperial family of Japan," I replied laconically.

Petrovitch was past surprise. If I had informed him that I was the Mikado in disguise, I think he would have taken it as a matter of course.

"This war is worth ten millions to me," he confessed hoarsely.

I shook my head with resignation.

"The price is too high. We must be enemies, not friends, I perceive."

The author of the war, who had regained his self-possession, did not blanch at these words.

"I regret it," he said with a courteous inclination.

"You have reason to."

He gave me a questioning glance.

"Up to the present I have been on the defensive," I explained. "I dislike violent measures. But from this moment I shall hold myself at liberty to use them."

"I am afraid I have gone rather too far," the promoter hesitated.

"You have drugged me. You have robbed me. You have murdered me."

"You are alive, however," he ventured to retort with an impudent smile.

"Unfortunately," I went on sternly, "in murdering me you exceeded your instructions."

"How——"

"I dreamed that I heard you tell your accomplice so," I put in, without giving him a chance to speak.

He ceased to meet my gaze.

"You are therefore not even a political criminal. You are a common felon. As such I warn you that I shall execute you without notice, and without reprieve."

The Russian scowled fiercely.

"We will see about that," he blustered. "I have a loaded revolver in my pocket."

I waved my hand scornfully.

"Undeceive yourself, George Petrovitch. I am not proposing a duel. I cannot be expected to fight with a condemned murderer. I sentence you to death—and may the Lord have mercy on your soul."

"By what right?" he demanded furiously.

"I am accredited by the Emperor of Japan to the Emperor of Russia. This house is Japanese soil. Farewell!"

Petrovitch rose from his chair, wavering between indignation and alarm.

"I shall defend myself!" he exclaimed, edging slowly toward the door.

"You will do better to confess yourself. Is there no prayer that you wish to say?"

The Russian smiled incredulously.

"You seem very confident," he sneered.

I saw that it was useless to try to rouse him to a sense of his peril. I pointed to the door, and pressed a knob on the wall.

The murderer made two steps from me, laid his fingers on the door-handle—and dropped dead instantly.

Chapter 25 A Change of Identity

I now approach the crucial portion of my narrative.

The incidents already dealt with, though not without a certain interest, perhaps, for those who value exact information about political events, are comparatively unimportant, and have been given here chiefly in order to inspire confidence in what follows.

At all events, their truth is not likely to be disputed, and I have not thought it necessary, therefore, to insist on every corroborative detail.

But I am now about to enter on what must be considered debatable ground.

I had taken the little house on the Alexander Quay, as the reader will have guessed, as a post of observation from which to watch the proceedings of the Russian Ministry of Marine, more particularly with regard to the fleet under the command of Admiral Rojestvensky.

It is my subsequent observations and discoveries which compel me, greatly to my regret, to give a direct contradiction to the gallant Admiral's version of what took place in the North Sea on the night of Trafalgar Day, 1904.

It is for that reason that I desire to exercise particular care in this part of my statement.

Such care is the more incumbent on me, inasmuch as I was requested by the British Government to furnish a confidential copy of my evidence in advance, for the use of the members of the international court which sat in Paris to inquire into this most mysterious affair.

The following chapters should be read, therefore, as the

sworn depositions of a witness, and not as the carelessly worded account of a journalist or popular historian.

The electrocution of the murderer, Petrovitch, already described, furnished me with a valuable opportunity which I was quick to seize.

I have not extenuated this act, and I will not defend it. I content myself with recording that this man had been the principal instrument in promoting the Russo-Japanese war, and the principal obstacle to peace. In this he was acting as the paid agent of a foreign Power, and was therefore guilty of high treason to his own country. On these grounds my execution of him, although irregular at the time, has since been formally ratified by the highest tribunal of the Russian Empire, the Imperial Council of State.

A justification which I value still more, consists in the fact that the removal of this man proved the turning point in the history of the war.

Within a month of his death I had the satisfaction to be made the medium of an informal overture for peace. The negotiations thus opened have proceeded with great secrecy, but before these lines meet the public eye, I have every hope that the calamitous struggle in Manchuria will have been suspended indefinitely.

To return:

Owing to the secret life led by the deceased man, it was some time before his absence from his usual haunts excited remark.

When it became evident that something must have happened to him, people were still slow to suspect that he had come to a violent end. Many persons believed that he had been ruined by the ill-success of the war, and had gone into hiding from his creditors. Others supposed that he had been secretly arrested.

Some of his fellow-plotters in the Russian capital imagined that he had fled to Germany to escape the penalty of his treason. In Germany, on the other hand, I afterward learned, he was supposed to have been sent to Siberia by order of the Czar.

For weeks the "Disappearance of M. Petrovitch" was the general topic of discussion in the newspapers and in private circles; but no one came near guessing the truth.

There was one person who must have divined from the first what had happened. But she held her tongue.

So far as I could gather from the reports which continued to reach me from Fauchette, the Princess Y— — had sunk into a lethargy after my evasion. She seemed to wish only to be left alone to brood, perhaps to mourn.

The only sign she gave was by depositing a wreath on the empty grave in the English cemetery, a wreath which bore the solitary word, "Remembrance."

In the meanwhile I had gratifying evidence that the loss of the chief conspirator had completely disorganized the schemes of the plotters in the Ministry of Marine.

My first proceeding, after disconnecting the powerful battery which I had installed in my house for the purpose of the execution, was to summon my assistant Breuil.

With his aid, the corpse was stripped and sewn up in a sheet, together with some heavy weights. In the middle of the night it was committed to the waters of the Neva, almost within sight and sound of the fleet.

The papers which we found in his clothes were not numerous or important. But there was one which I thought worth preserving.

It was a passport, made out in the name of the deceased, issued by the Russian Foreign Office, and viséd by the German Ambassador. This passport I still have in my possession.

I now disclosed to my assistant a plan which had been in my own mind for some time, though, true to my principle of never making an unnecessary confidence, I had not previously mentioned it to him.

"I have decided," I told him, "to assume the personality of Petrovitch."

Breuil stared at me in consternation. It is only fair to say that he had not been with me very long.

I could see that some objection was trembling on the tip of his tongue. He had learned, however, that I expect my staff not to criticize, but to obey.

"You may speak," I said indulgently, "if you have anything to say."

"I was about to remark, sir, that you are not in the least like Petrovitch."

"Think again," I said mildly.

He gave me an intelligent look.

"You are much about the same height!" he exclaimed.

"Exactly."

"But his friends, who see him every day—surely they cannot be deceived? And then his business—his correspondence—but perhaps you are able to feign handwriting?"

I smiled. The good Breuil had passed from one extreme to the other. Instead of doubting me, he was crediting me too much.

I proceeded to explain.

"No, as you very properly suggest, I could not hope to deceive Petrovitch's friends, nor can I imitate his hand. But remember, that in a few days Petrovitch will have disappeared. What will have become of him, do you suppose?"

Breuil was still puzzled. I had to make my meaning still plainer.

"He will be in concealment—that is to say, in disguise."

Breuil threw up his hands in a gesture of admiration.

"As the disguised Petrovitch I may manage to pass very well, more particularly as I shall be meeting people who have never seen the real Petrovitch."

Breuil did not quite understand this last observation.

"I am going," I exclaimed, "on board the Baltic Fleet."

"Sir, you are magnificent!"

I frowned down his enthusiasm. Compliments are compliments only when they come from those who pay us, not from those whom we pay.

"Go and procure me the uniform of a superintendent of naval stores. And ascertain for me where Captain Vassileffsky usually passes his evenings."

Captain Vassileffsky was the naval officer who had been present on the occasion when I was drugged at Petrovitch's table.

Chapter 26 Trapped

The clock was striking eight as I entered the restaurant of the Two-Headed Eagle, in the seaport of Revel on the Gulf of Finland, about a week after the mysterious disappearance of Petrovitch had become the talk of Petersburg.

Picking out a table at which an officer in the uniform of a Russian naval captain was already seated, I went up to it, and sat down in front of him with the formal bow prescribed by etiquette in the circumstances.

The ships intended to sail to the relief of Port Arthur were lying at this time some at Revel and others at Libau on the Baltic. From time to time their departure was officially announced for a certain date, reviews were held, and one or two preliminary trips had been undertaken.

But each time some unseen obstacle was interposed, and M. Auguste continued to draw his weekly stipend.

Nevertheless it was beginning to be evident that the game of see-saw could not go on forever. Autumn was approaching, the nation was becoming impatient, and the scoffs of the foreign press were severely galling the naval pride of Russia.

I had picked up a certain amount of information in the capital itself, where a great number of the officers were on leave. But I wished to get in direct touch with the one man who, I believed, was most likely to be in the confidence of Petrovitch, and, finding there was no chance of his coming to Petersburg, I had been obliged to make the journey to Revel.

Vassileffsky acknowledged my bow with cordiality, at the same time fixing his dark, wicked eyes on me with a look which I well understood.

I was wearing the uniform which I had ordered my assistant to provide me with, and the Captain had been quick to take note of it.

It may be said that the most valuable part of a naval officer's income in Russia is derived from the peculation of government stores. To carry on this lucrative system of plunder there is always a good understanding between officials of the Stores Department and the combatant officers.

Captain Vassileffsky now studied my face like a man expecting to receive some proposal of the kind. I, on my side, made it my business to say as little as possible to him till dinner was over.

Then I called for a magnum of champagne, and invited my companion to fill a tumbler.

He did so readily enough, and I gave him the toast,

"To the Emperor who wishes us well!"

Vassileffsky started, and gave me a penetrating look.

He did not venture to put a question to me, however, and contented himself with drinking the toast in silence.

Determined not to say anything as long as the Captain remained sober, I plied him with champagne in increasing quantities, while taking as little as possible myself.

On his side Vassileffsky was equally reserved. He saw, of course, that I had a special object in courting his friendship, and was cunning enough to let me make the first advance.

As soon as I thought the wine had had time to confuse his faculties, I leaned forward and whispered,

"I've got something to say to you about Petrovitch."

The Captain looked at me eagerly.

"Do you know where he is?"

"Not so loud. Yes. He has had to disguise himself."

I spoke in a muffled tone, which Vassileffsky imitated in his response.

"Where is he? I want to see him very badly."

"I know. He wants to see you. He is here in Revel."

"In Revel! Isn't that dangerous?"

"It would be if he weren't so well disguised. You, yourself, wouldn't know him."

Vassileffsky looked incredulous.

"I bet I should."

"Done with you! What in?"

"A dozen magnums."

"Pay for them, then. *I'm Petrovitch.*"

The Captain started, shook himself, and peered drunkenly into my face.

"I don't believe it."

"Read that then."

I drew out the passport, and spread it before him. The Russian spelled his way through it, and nodded solemnly at the end.

"Yes, that's all right. You must be Petrovitch, I suppose. But you don't look like him."

"Didn't I tell you I was disguised. I had to clear out in a hurry. Some one's been denouncing me to Nicholas."

Vassileffsky looked frightened. His eye sought the door, as though he no longer felt at ease in my company.

"You needn't be afraid," I assured him. "No one suspects you."

"Well, what do you want?" he asked sullenly.

"I want you to take me on board your ship."

An angry frown crossed his face.

"You want me to hide you from the police!"

"Nonsense. The police are all right. They want me to get away. They could have put their hands on me long ago if they had wanted to."

"Then why have you come here?"

"I told you. I want to have a talk with you about our plans."

"The plan is all right. But I want to know when we're to sail."

"I'm doing all I can. It's only a question of weeks now."

Vassileffsky looked hard at me again, bent across the table, and whispered a word which I failed to understand.

Something in his face warned me that it was a password. I recovered myself from my momentary confusion and smiled.

"The word's changed," I said with an air of authority. "It's *North Sea* and *Canal*."

The Russian seemed satisfied.

"Well," he said, stumbling to his feet, "if we're going on board we'd better go."

"Don't forget the magnums," I put in, as I rose in my turn.

The reckoning was settled, and the champagne ordered to follow us down to the boat.

Vassileffsky nearly lost his footing as we got out into the fresh air, and caught hold of my arm.

"You'll have to lead me," he said, speaking thickly. "Straight along the street, and down the first turning on the quay."

We walked along, arm-in-arm, my companion appearing

to become more helpless every minute.

As we emerged from the narrow lane which conducted us to the waterside, the lights of the harbor burst into view. There on the tide lay a long line of stately battleships, cruisers and dark, low-lying torpedo boats, their riding lights flashing and twinkling in a thousand reflections on the waves.

A drunken hail from the Captain was responded to by a respectful hail from a Russian petty officer, who was lounging at the head of some stone steps.

He came forward and assisted his commanding officer down and into the launch which waited below. I followed, and the bottles of champagne were handed in afterward.

Vassileffsky seized the tiller with more energy than he had seemed capable of, and headed the launch for a great battleship, the *Beresina*.

In a few minutes we were alongside. A smart landing stage and ladder brought us up on to the deck, and as soon as our feet touched it, Captain Vassileffsky, suddenly drawing himself up, said in distinct and sober tones,

"Consider yourself under arrest, if you please——"

I was a prisoner on board a Russian man-of-war!

Chapter 27 The Baltic Fleet

Fortunately I am accustomed to face emergencies without losing my presence of mind.

The manner of Vassileffsky had prepared me for some display of suspicion on his part, though I hardly anticipated his procedure would be so theatrical.

Fixing him with my sternest look, I responded,

"Captain Vassileffsky, I do not think you quite understand what you are doing. I will talk to you in the morning, when you are more yourself."

He drew back, considerably disconcerted.

"Very well, I will listen to what you have to say in the morning. In the meantime you will be under a guard."

I shrugged my shoulders with a disdainful smile.

"Be good enough to let me see my quarters," I said.

More and more abashed, the Captain summoned one of his officers, and gave him some instructions.

"Follow me, sir," said the lieutenant. I walked after him with perfect self-possession.

"I do not wish to make a fuss to-night, as Captain Vassileffsky is not himself," I said haughtily, as we drew out of hearing. "But you will understand that unless I receive an apology in the morning, I shall complain to his majesty the Czar, by whose orders I am here."

The lieutenant looked badly frightened.

"It is not my fault, as you can see, sir. I am only obeying orders. Will you accept my own berth for the night, sir?"

I thanked him and entered a small, comfortably-fitted state-room. With profuse apologies, he turned the key and left me to my own reflections.

I slept soundly, rocked by the tide of the Finland Gulf.

In the morning my jailer came to wake me.

"Captain Vassileffsky presents his compliments, and asks you to breakfast with him in his cabin, in half an hour."

This message was a welcome proof to me that my bluff had produced the desired effect. I accepted the invitation as if it was a matter of course.

I dressed, and went to the cabin where Vassileffsky awaited me.

"Are we friends or foes this morning?" I called out with a good-humored laugh, as I greeted him.

The Russian looked dull and nervous.

"I hope all will be well," he muttered. "Let us have something to eat before we talk."

He might have said, something to drink, for his own breakfast was mainly of champagne. I, myself, made a point of eating heartily, and drank only coffee.

"Now, Vassileffsky," I said in authoritative tones, "to business. First of all, you want some money."

It was a guess, but a fairly safe one. Without waiting for the astonished man to reply, I took out my pocket-book.

"How much can you do with till the fleet sails?" I asked, still in the same matter-of-fact tone.

Fairly nonplussed, the Captain blurted out,

"I should like two thousand."

I shook my head.

"I can let you have only a thousand now, but you shall have the balance this day week." I counted the thousand rubles, and handed them to him. "They are grumbling, rather, in Berlin over the expense."

It was, of course, my object to give Vassileffsky no opening for a cross-examination, but to take it for granted that we were on confidential terms.

At the word "Berlin" he opened his eyes pretty wide.

"Does this money come from Germany?" he exclaimed, half-withdrawing his hand.

I affected surprise in my turn.

"You have not received any information at all, apparently! My message must have miscarried. Didn't the Princess see you?"

Vassileffsky looked still more surprised. His demeanor taught me a good deal. I saw that Petrovitch had not trusted him very far. The financier had evidently kept all the threads of the intrigue in his own hands, as far as possible.

So much the better, I reflected. His removal would disorganize matters even more thoroughly than I had ventured to hope.

"What Princess?" the Captain asked.

"The Princess Y——, of course."

He brightened up a little, as though this name, at all events, was familiar.

"No, she has not been here."

"One can never trust these women," I muttered aloud. "She has not been at all the same since the death of her Englishman."

"Of Sterling, do you mean?"

"Yes. You heard of it, I suppose?"

Vassileffsky grinned.

"Rather sudden, wasn't it?"

I smiled meaningly, as I retorted,

"You remember he fainted rather unexpectedly that night he dined with me."

A look of relief broke out on Vassileffsky's face, as I thus referred to an incident which he naturally supposed could be known only to Petrovitch.

"My dear fellow, I beg a thousand pardons for my stupid conduct last night," he burst out. "But you must admit that your disguise is extraordinary."

"Not a word!" I returned. "It is always better to err on the side of distrust. Besides, I wished to spend a night on your ship in any case. Your crew can be thoroughly depended on, if I am any judge."

"They would bombard the Tower of London, if I gave the word," boasted Vassileffsky.

It is extraordinary how widely the belief prevails on the Continent of Europe that the London Tower is still a fortress, charged with the protection of the British capital.

"At all events, they will not be frightened by the sight of the Union Jack?" I returned.

The Russian officer gave me an alarmed glance.

"You do not mean—you are not asking us to fire on the British fleet?"

"No, no," I reassured him.

"Ah, that is all right. For the moment I confess you frightened me. They say we shall have to pass Admiral Beresford!"

"What are you prepared to do?" I asked, concealing my deep interest in the reply.

Vassileffsky's manner became slightly reproachful.

"You did not bargain with me to attack an armed ship,"

he said in the tone of one who reminds another of his agreement. "It was understood that we were to attack merchantmen, like the Vladivostockers."

At last I had a direct confirmation of my suspicions.

"And what is the tone of the fleet generally?" I inquired.

"I have done my best to make them all of the same mind. They will do their best, depend on it. I think there will be a few English vessels mysteriously lost at sea during the next two or three months! The prize courts cannot always be depended on."

By an effort I restrained my indignation at these atrocious hints. The Baltic Fleet was about to seek the open sea, secretly intending to miss no chance of sinking a British merchantman that should be unlucky enough to cross its path.

It was with a feeling of chagrin that I perceived it would be useless to send any message to Lord Bedale of what was in preparation. On certain subjects the British people are deaf and blind. They believe that all foreign statesmen are as high-minded as a Gladstone, and all foreign officials as scrupulous and truthful as the Chevalier Bayard himself.

Captain Vassileffsky continued,

"Our men are badly scared by reports of the Japanese plans. It is supposed that they have torpedo boats lurking in the English ports. Hull is said to be full of them."

"Why, Hull?"

Vassileffsky gave me a wink.

"Hull is the great fishing center. Whole fleets of traders come out from there to the fishing banks in the North Sea. We are going to stir them up a bit."

The outlines of the plot became every moment more clear.

"On what pretext?" I asked.

The Russian answered me without noticing that I was not so well informed as himself.

"Oh, we shall find pretexts enough, you bet. For one thing, we shall signal them to clear out of the way, and when they have their trawl nets down and can't move! That will be lively. There will be a collision or two, I shouldn't wonder."

"But isn't that against the rule of the road?"

Though not a seaman, I had always heard that a vessel in motion is bound to avoid one that is at rest. I knew, moreover, that a steamship was bound to make way for a sailing vessel.

Vassileffsky cursed the rule of the road.

"It will be a question of evidence," he exclaimed. "My word against a dirty fisherman's. What do you say?"

I pretended to be thoroughly satisfied. Still, knowing what I did of the Russian character, I had some hope that the Captain was boasting in order to impress me, and that he would not really dare to run down a British vessel within reach of the shores of England.

Our conversation was interrupted by a gun.

As the report died away, a junior officer ran down the companionway, helter-skelter, and burst into the cabin.

"Something's up, sir," he cried to his commander. "They are signaling from the Admiral's ship."

Vassileffsky darted up the steps and on to the bridge, and I followed.

The Baltic fleet presented a striking spectacle. Every vessel was busily reporting the signals from the flag ship, the launches were dashing to and fro, and there was every sign of bustle and activity.

The signal officer read out Admiral Rojestvensky's order:

"The fleet will proceed to Libau to-day *en route* to the East. Anchors will be weighed at noon. By order of the Czar."

M. Auguste had failed me at last!

With the frightful boasts of Vassileffsky still ringing in my ears, I felt that I must make one effort to stay its departure.

"This news compels me to return to Petersburg immediately," I told the Captain. "Have the goodness to put me ashore at once."

For a moment or two the Russian made no answer. I glanced at him curiously.

His face had gone suddenly livid. His limbs were trembling. He gave me the dull look of a man stupefied by fear.

"The Japanese!" he ejaculated in a thick voice.

I seized him by the arm.

"Are you pretending?" I whispered.

He gave me a savage glance.

"It's true!" he said. "Those devils will be up to something. It's all over with the fleet. No one believes we shall ever see Port Arthur."

Grave and pre-occupied, I went ashore and caught a fast train to Petersburg.

It was late when I got to the little house on the Alexander Quay. The faithful Breuil received me with a serious face.

"Fauchette is here," he announced.

"Fauchette?"

"Yes. She has some news for you."

"Let me see her."

I strode in front to my study, where I was immediately joined by the maid, who appeared not a little alarmed.

I never like to see my assistants agitated.

"Sit down, my good girl," I said soothingly. "Do not be afraid; I know what pains you take to serve me. Now, what is it?"

"Madame has dismissed me."

I had feared as much.

"On what grounds?"

"She gave none, except that she was leaving home."

I pricked up my ears.

"Did she tell you where she was going?"

"Yes, to her estates in the country."

"It was a lie, I suppose. She had come to suspect you, had she not?"

"Since Monsieur's escape, I fear yes."

"And have you ascertained — — ?"

"The Princess has left Petersburg by the midday train for — —"

"For?" I broke in impatiently.

"For Berlin."

I rang the bell. Breuil appeared.

"Have you got the tickets?" I asked.

"Yes, sir."

"And my dress as a pilot of the Kiel Canal?"

"It is packed."

"And what time does the next train leave?"

"In two hours from now."

"Good. And now, my children, we will have supper."

As the really exciting moment of the protracted struggle drew near, I summoned all my energies to meet it.

I alighted in Berlin armed only with two weapons, the passport made out in the name of Petrovitch, and a fairly accurate knowledge of the schemes, or at all events the hopes, of the German Government.

From the first beginning of my long investigation, all the clues I had picked up had led steadily in one direction.

The great disorganized Empire of the Czar's, with its feeble-willed autocrat, its insubordinate grand dukes, its rival ministers pulling different ways, and its greedy officials whose country was their pocket, had been silently and steadily enfolded in the invisible web of German statecraft.

The brilliant personality of Wilhelm II had magnetized the vacillating, timorous Nicholas. Count Bülow had courted the Russian Foreign Office with the assiduous arts of a lover, and his wooing had been crowned by complete success. Through Petrovitch the grand dukes had been indirectly bribed, and the smaller fry like M. Auguste had been bought outright. Even the Army and Navy had been cajoled, or bought, or terrorized by pretended revelations of Japanese designs.

Russia had become a supple implement in the hands of the German Kaiser, the sovereign who for nearly twenty years had been striving toward one goal by a hundred different crooked paths.

It was evident that the unexplained disappearance of Petrovitch must have struck consternation into his employers. I suspected that the Princess Y— — had been summoned to Berlin to throw light on the event, and possibly to be furnished with instructions which would enable her to take over the dead man's work.

My position was now peculiarly difficult. I wished to get in touch with the principals for whom Petrovitch had acted, but to avoid, if possible, meeting any one who had known him personally.

Above all, I was determined not to risk an encounter with Sophia. She knew that I was still alive, and I feared that her feminine intuition, quickened by love, would penetrate through whatever disguise I might adopt.

Under these circumstances I decided to begin by approaching Herr Finkelstein, the head of the imperial Secret Service in Berlin.

This man was an old crony of mine. While a magnificent organizer of espionage, he was a poor observer himself, and I had already succeeded on one occasion in imposing myself on him under a false identity.

I had brought with me the papers which I had obtained by bribery from the police agent Rostoy, representing me as an inspector in the secret police of the Russian Empire.

Wearing my pilot's dress, but carrying these and other papers in my pocket, I presented myself at Finkelstein's office, and asked to see him.

I was shown in first, as I had expected, to Finkelstein's secretary, who asked me my business.

"I can tell that only to the Herr Superintendent himself," I said.

"If you will let him know that I have just come from Petersburg, I am sure he will receive me."

The secretary seemed to think so too. He went straight into his chief's room and came out immediately to fetch me in.

As soon as I found myself alone with the head of the German service, I said quietly,

"I have brought you a message from M. Petrovitch."

"Petrovitch!" exclaimed the Superintendent, surprised out of his usual caution. "But he is dead!"

"You have been misinformed," I replied in an assured tone.

Finkelstein looked at me searchingly.

"My informant does not often make mistakes," he observed.

"The Princess is deceived this time, however," was my retort.

It was a fresh surprise for the Superintendent.

"The Princess! Then you know?" He broke off short, conscious that he was making an admission.

"The Princess Y— — having left Petersburg, it was natural to suppose that she had come here to consult you," I answered modestly, not wishing to appear too well informed.

Finkelstein frowned.

"You have not yet told me who you are," he reminded me.

I produced the forged papers.

"I am an inspector attached to the Third Section, as you will see. I must inform you, however, that I am not here with the knowledge of my superiors."

The German gave a glance at the papers, which were similar to others which he must have had presented to him from time to time.

"That is all satisfactory," he said, as he returned them to me. "But you say that you have a message from M. Petrovitch?"

"He had no opportunity of giving me any but this," I responded, producing the passport.

This time Finkelstein seemed really satisfied.

"It is clear that you know something about him, at least," he remarked. "I will listen to what you have to say."

"M. Petrovitch is confined in Schlüsselburg."

The name of the dreaded fortress, the last home of so many political prisoners, caused Finkelstein a shock.

"*Gott im Himmel!* You don't say so! How did he get there? Tell me everything."

"He does not know from what quarter the blow came. The only person he can think of who might have denounced him is the Princess herself."

"The Princess Y——?"

"Exactly."

The German looked incredulous.

"But they were hand in glove. The Princess was his best agent."

"True. Unfortunately there is always one source of danger where a woman is concerned—she cannot control her affections. It appears that M. Petrovitch ordered her to remove a certain Englishman, a spy of some kind, who was giving trouble, and Madame Y—— was attached to the fellow. She carried out her orders, but M. Petrovitch fears that she has taken revenge on him."

Finkelstein gave a superior smile.

"I can dispose of that suspicion," he said confidently. "The Princess did *not* carry out her orders. The man you speak of—who is the most dangerous and unprincipled scoundrel in the world—has escaped, and we have lost all trace of him."

It was my turn to show surprise and alarm.

"What you tell me is appalling! I ought to see the Princess as soon as possible. If what she says is true, it must be the Englishman who has brought about Petrovitch's arrest."

"He is no Englishman," the Superintendent returned. "He is an American, a Pole, a Frenchman, whatever you please. That man has been at the bottom of all the troubles in Europe for the last twenty years. I have employed him myself, sometimes, so I ought to know something about him."

I listened with an interest that was not feigned to this character of myself. It was, all the same, a lie that Finkelstein had ever employed me; on the contrary, I had been called in by his imperial master to check his work.

"Then what is to be done?" I asked, as the German finished speaking. "M. Petrovitch sent me here to warn you against the Princess, and to demand your influence to secure his release."

"That will be a difficult matter. I shall have to consult the Minister. In the meantime, where can I find you?"

I mentioned the name of a hotel.

"And the Princess Y——? Where can I see her?"

"I expect that she has left for Kiel," said the Superintendent. "She has volunteered to carry out the plan originally proposed by Petrovitch."

"Then in that case you will not require my services?" I said, with an air of being disappointed. "M. Petrovitch thought you might find me useful in his place."

"I must consult others before I can say anything as to

that," was the cautious reply.

He added rather grudgingly,

"I did not know M. Petrovitch myself, you see. It was thought better that he should not come to Berlin."

This statement relieved me of a great anxiety. I now saw my way to take a bolder line.

"So I understood, sir. But I did not venture to approach his majesty except through you."

Finkelstein started again, and gave me a new look of curiosity.

"Who authorized you to mention the Emperor?"

I tried to play the part of a man who has made an unintentional slip.

"I spoke too quickly. Petrovitch informed me—that is to say, I supposed—" I broke down in feigned confusion.

I knew inquisitiveness to be the Superintendent's besetting sin, and, up to a certain point, I had an interest in tempting him on.

"You appear to be more in the confidence of M. Petrovitch than you are willing to admit," he said sagely. "Up to the present you have not explained how he came to make you his messenger."

I leaned back with a faint smile.

"I imagine you are quite astute enough to guess my secret, if you choose, Herr Finkelstein. But you must excuse me if I am a little careful whom I trust, especially after the behavior of Princess Y——."

"You are M. Petrovitch himself! Of course! I thought as much all along," Finkelstein said with a smile of triumph. "Well, you are certainly right to be cautious; but, as you see, it is not easy to deceive an old hand like myself."

"At all events you will be at least equally cautious, I hope. What you tell me about this international spy being still at large has disturbed me a good deal, I confess."

"Make your mind easy," the German returned with a patronizing air. "We are in Berlin here, not in Petersburg. This gentleman will not venture within my reach, I assure you."

I professed every satisfaction with this guarantee, and took my leave.

Chapter 29 An Imperial Fanatic

I was now to face Wilhelm II.

It was solely for this purpose that I had come to Berlin. But I knew the great advantage of getting myself vouched for in advance by a third party, and therefore I had been anxious to convince Finkelstein of my identity in the first place, so that his master might accept me without inquiry as to whether I was the man I claimed to be.

I dined quietly in my hotel, a small tavern in a back street. It was getting late, and I was on the point of going to bed, when I heard the noise of a motor rushing up and stopping suddenly outside the little inn.

An aide-de-camp burst in upon me.

"Your name, sir?" he demanded in a whisper.

"Petrovitch," I replied in the same tone.

"Come this way, if you please."

In less than a minute I was seated in the car, which was dashing at a really dangerous pace through the nearly deserted streets.

"I am taking you to Potsdam," was all the explanation my companion thought necessary.

It did not take us long to reach the famous palace of Frederick the Great, which the growth of Berlin has almost turned into a suburban residence.

My conductor brought me past all the sentries and servants, and led me down some steps into what seemed to be a subterranean hall. It was decorated with statues and paintings of the ancestors of Wilhelm II., together with weapons, suits of armor, and banners of the successive periods in which they lived.

But the most striking object in the hall or crypt—for it might have been either—was a trophy erected on a species of altar at one end, exhibiting a variety of crowns.

At the foot were a number of small coronets, representing those worn by the former Margraves of Brandenburg, in whom the Hohenzollern family took its rise. Above were ranged the crowns of the Kings of Prussia, that of Frederick the Great being in the center. Still higher rose the three imperial crowns of Germany, those of William I., Frederick III., and the present Emperor. And then, right on the summit, came a still more gorgeous object, whose like I had never seen before.

It was a colossal miter, somewhat after the fashion of the Papal tiara, wrought out of pure gold, thickly studded with great pearls, and surmounted by a cross.

But I had barely time to notice this singular display. As my guide left me on the threshold of the hall, I was aware that I stood in the presence of the German Emperor.

This extraordinary monarch, whose great and far-reaching views are combined with a type of extravagance which has long made him looked upon as the *enfant terrible* of Europe, was about to teach me a new side of his character.

He received me seated in a small ivory chair like a throne, and attired in a garment of pontifical design.

"Advance, M. Petrovitch," he commanded in a loud voice.

As I stood in front of him, he said theatrically,

"I receive you in the Hall of the Hohenzollerns. You see around you the sacred memorials of the family which Providence has raised up to be the saviors of Europe, and the future rulers of the world."

In response to this invitation I took a longer and more comprehensive view of the various objects already described. The Kaiser condescended to point some of them out to me with a long two-handed sword which he held.

I began to suspect seriously that the megalomania which has always formed one of Wilhelm's characteristic traits, was overpowering his good sense.

"M. Petrovitch," my august cicerone proceeded, "you see there the crowns which have been won and worn by my illustrious and never-to-be-forgotten ancestors. Can you guess the meaning of the diadem above—which I have designed myself?

"That," declared the last and most remarkable of the Hohenzollerns, "is intended to be worn by that member of my Family who shall be called by the united voice of the other sovereigns to the supreme world monarchy. It is destined to be our Planetary Crown."

I bowed in stupefaction. The Kaiser seemed pleased with the impression he had made.

"And now," he said, "since it is necessary that I should be sure of you before I trust you with my plans, kneel down."

I knelt, feeling as if I were in a dream. Wilhelm II. solemnly held out the hilt of his two-handed sword:—

"You swear to yield faith, loyalty and utter obedience now and henceforth to Almighty God, and the Head of the Hohenzollerns!"

It being impossible to refuse the oath in the circumstances, I kissed the sword, with a mental reservation.

Wilhelm II. surprised me by thereupon laying it across my shoulders.

"I dub thee knight of the Sacred Order of the Hohenzollerns! Arise."

I got up, thoroughly confused. The Emperor invited me to be seated, and proceeded to deliver a harangue—for it was nothing less.

"Bismarck had not sufficient genius to see the destiny of the Hohenzollerns. With the vision of a mere German Junker, he looked on Russia as the enemy.

"It is I who have changed all that. I have taught the Czar to look to me for guidance and protection. Should the present revolutionary movement become dangerous, I shall march at the head of my army to the rescue, and reinstate the Romanoffs as my vassals.

"The only obstacle in the path of the Hohenzollerns is an island which two of my Army Corps could subdue in a fortnight. But in order to invade it with safety, I must have France on my side.

"It is for this end that I have been working. France cherishes a grudge against me because of the glorious exploits of my immortal grandfather. Moreover, my uncle, Edward VII., has contrived to win the friendship of the Republicans.

"But France is the ally of Russia, and if Russia is attacked, France must draw the sword on her behalf.

"You understand?—with the first shot which is fired by a British warship on the Russian flag, I shall be able to invade England."

I understood indeed. Briefly and plainly Wilhelm II. had summed up the result of my own inquiries and reasonings.

"It is you," the Emperor proceeded, "who have undertaken to secure this result."

I bowed, intensely desirous to know exactly what it was that Petrovitch had pledged himself to do.

"I have just rewarded you for the services you have already rendered, by admitting you to my Family Order, an order which I intend shall take precedence of the Golden Fleece, and even the Garter. Should you carry out your present task to my satisfaction I shall consider no reward too great for you."

I trembled as I listened to this wild vaporing. If such were the private thoughts of the Kaiser, no wonder some of his public utterances smacked of the visionary.

I could not doubt that he was thoroughly in earnest. Long brooding on the greatness of his ancestors, and his own importance as the sole European ruler who has kings for his satellites, had filled him with the fanatical spirit of a Mohammed or a Hildebrand. He believed, firmly and sincerely believed, that Providence had called him to the sovereignty of the globe, and authorized him to sweep every rival out of his path.

"Your majesty overwhelms me," I murmured. "Consider, sire, that to be your servant is in itself an honor so great that no other reward is necessary."

The Kaiser smiled graciously.

"Well, now, M. *de* Petrovitch— —" his majesty emphasized the particle by way of reminding me that I was now a knight of the important Order of Hohenzollern—"let us discuss your next step."

I seized the opportunity to obtain the information I was so anxious to secure.

"I should feel it presumptuous to enter into anything like a discussion with you, sire. If your majesty will be gracious enough to impart your criticism on my proposal?"

Wilhelm II. looked at me as though he found me to be a person of much good sense.

"Your idea, my dear de Petrovitch, as I understand it, is to provoke the British to reprisals by some outrage on the part of the Baltic Fleet during its passage to the Far East.

"Unfortunately, as you must see, the British are determined not to be provoked. Remember what has been done already. You have captured and sunk their ships, in violation of international law; you have sent out volunteer cruisers from the Black Sea in defiance of treaties, and turned back their mail steamers with government stores on board.

"What has been the result? The English Government has complained to yours; the Czar has ordered explanations to be given, and the thing has blown over.

"This time there must be something more than that. There must be something which cannot be explained away. We must if possible place Nicholas II., as well as Great Britain, in a position from which neither can retreat without loss of honor.

"To this end it is necessary that the Baltic Fleet should commit an act of war, and that the Czar should be convinced that the provocation has come from the English side. Do you understand?"

I recalled the hints dropped by Captain Vassileffsky at Revel.

"Your majesty has been informed perhaps that I have caused the officers and men of the Fleet to believe that they will find Japanese torpedo boats lying in wait for them among the English fishing vessels in the North Sea. In consequence, they will be ready to fire without waiting to see if the torpedo boats are really there, especially if the fishermen fail to retire as the

Fleet approaches."

The Kaiser shook his head.

"All that is leaving too much to chance, my good de Petrovitch. What is required is something more positive. In short, the torpedo boats must really be there."

I lifted my eyes to his.

"There is not a Japanese torpedo boat within ten thousand miles of the North Sea, unfortunately."

Wilhelm II. smiled a meaning smile.

"If that is all, we must so far forget the duties of neutrality as to allow the friends of Japan to procure a craft suitable for the purpose from our dockyard at Kiel."

As the full extent of this audacious plot was laid bare before my eyes I had a difficulty in believing in its reality.

I was obliged to remind myself of some of the maneuvres which have marked German statecraft in the recent past, of the forgeries and "reinsurance" treaties of Bismarck, of the patronage extended to Abdul Hamid, of the secret intrigue that brought about the disasters of Greece.

If I had had any scepticism left, the Emperor would have dispelled it by the clear and business-like explanations which followed.

His majesty produced a chart of the North Sea, showing the coasts of Great Britain and Germany, with the Kiel Canal and so forth. Half-way between the opposite shores a dotted outline marked the situation of the great shoals which attract the fish, and from which the harvests of the sea are gathered by the brave and industrious toilers of Grimsby, Hull, and many another port.

From the northern point of Denmark, two lines in red ink were drawn right down the map to where the North Sea narrows into the Straits of Dover.

The first of these lines was fairly direct, passing about thirty miles to the eastward of the great fishing grounds.

The second line took a wide curve to the west, and crossed right over the center of a shoal marked "Dogger Bank."

The Kaiser proceeded to explain.

"This is a duplicate of the charts used by the pilots of the North Sea. I have offered my brother Nicholas as a special favor the services of German pilots, and they will board the vessels of the Baltic Fleet as soon as it leaves Danish waters.

"As you see, the right course would take the fleet a long way off the English fishing-boats. But the pilots who go on board will receive secret orders at the last moment to take the Russian ships over the Dogger Bank, and, if possible, into the very midst of any fishing fleet that may be there.

"Then all that is required is that you should be on the spot, and should fire the first shot from the midst of the fishing-boats."

I endeavored to preserve a calm demeanor.

"May I suggest to your majesty that the presence of a torpedo boat among them is likely to arouse suspicion beforehand. The English sailors have keen eyes."

"I have thought of that. It will be necessary for you to have a submarine."

"A submarine, sire!"

"Certainly. I have had six submarine torpedo boats built by my own designs at Kiel since this war broke out, for use in defending the approaches to the Canal.

"These boats are now lying in the inner harbor, all fitted out and ready for sea.

"You will take one, with a crew of your own, whom you must enlist secretly, and slip out through the Canal into the North Sea.

"You will proceed, keeping under the surface, till you reach the Dogger Bank, and find yourself among the trawl nets of the English fishermen.

"There you will wait till such time as the Russian ships come up.

"As soon as the right moment has arrived, you will rise to

the surface and discharge a torpedo. As soon as you have drawn the fire of the Russians, and have seen an English fishing-boat struck, you can go beneath the surface again, and make the best of your way back to Kiel."

"Your plan is perfection itself, sire!" I exclaimed with an admiration which was not wholly pretended, since the idea really was not lacking in cleverness.

The Kaiser nodded good-humoredly.

"The Russians will never be persuaded they were not attacked first, and the English will never pass over such an outrage in their own waters," his majesty remarked complacently. "Lord Charles Beresford will do the rest."

"I am ready to carry out your orders, sire. All I require is an authority to take the submarine from Kiel."

The Kaiser frowned.

"Have you had any authority from me for anything you have done up to the present, sir?" he demanded harshly.

As an answer in the negative was clearly expected, I gave it.

"Understand me, M. de Petrovitch, I repose every confidence in you; but I should not have held this conversation with any man, even my Chancellor, if I thought it could ever be used against me. If I gave you the authority you ask for, I should not be able to deny that I had ever employed you, in case of trouble."

"Then you propose, sire——?"

"I intend you to take this vessel secretly, without authority from me or from any one else."

"And if I am caught in the act of taking it? If any of the naval authorities question my movements?"

"You will not be caught. Your movements will not be questioned. I can assure you of so much."

"I thank you, sire. That is quite sufficient."

I retired from the imperial presence, though not, as I have had some reason to suspect, from the imperial observation. In other words, I felt pretty well convinced that there would be a watch on my movements till my task was over.

The same aide-de-camp awaited me outside the Hall of the Hohenzollerns, and carried me back to my obscure hotel with the same speed and silence as he had brought me.

The next morning I arose to find the papers filled with the news of the departure of the Baltic Fleet from Libau.

The Russian Admiral, as if in obedience to the secret promptings of Berlin, was reported as having issued a preposterous and illegal warning that he should fire on any ship of any nation that presumed to venture within reach of his guns. I could not help wondering what would be thought of this proclamation in the British Admiralty.

There being no more for me to do in Berlin, I took the first train to Kiel, the Portsmouth of Germany. Kiel itself, it will be remembered, stands at the Baltic end of the famous canal which the present Kaiser has had constructed for his warships to pass out to the North Sea without going around Denmark.

It was late when I arrived, but I determined to lose no time in seeing how far the secret orders of the Kaiser extended.

Accordingly, as soon as I had dined, I went out and took my way toward the government dockyard.

The entrance to the dockyard was guarded by a sentry with fixed bayonet. Behind him I saw a large iron gate which appeared to be heavily barred, with a small postern at one side, which was also closed.

I advanced toward the sentry, expecting every moment to hear a challenge ring out. To my genuine astonishment, nothing of the kind occurred. The sentry did not pay the slightest attention to me, but went on pacing to and fro as though I had been wearing a cap of invisibility.

I went up to the postern door, and tried the handle. It opened at a touch, and I found myself alone in the deserted dockyard.

For some time I groped my way forward by the light of the few scattered electric lights, till I reached the edge of a large basin which appeared to communicate with the outer harbor of Kiel.

Turning the opposite way, I went along the edge of the wharf, picking my way among timber balks, stacks of iron sheeting, chains, ropes, and all the other things that are found scattered about a naval dockyard.

At the head of the great basin I found a lock giving access to a small inner dock, in which a number of vessels were moored.

I made my way around, searching everywhere for the vessels I had been told I should find.

At last, in the farthest and most secluded corner, I perceived a row of small craft, shaped much like a shark, with a long narrow tube or funnel rising up from the center of each.

They lay low in the water, without being submerged. Alone among the shipping they carried no riding-lights. They appeared dark, silent, and deserted.

Almost unconsciously I ran my eye along them, counting them as they lay. Suddenly I was aroused to keen attention.

One—two—three—four—five. The Kaiser had assured

me that I should find six submarines to choose from!

I counted once more with straining eyes.

One—two—three—four—five.

One of the mysterious craft had been taken away!

Chapter 31 The Kiel Canal

It was impossible to resist the conclusion suggested by the absence of the sixth submarine.

I was not the only person who had been authorized, or rather instructed, to carry out the design against the Baltic Fleet. My august employer had thought it better to have two strings to his bow.

Who, then, was the person by whom I had been anticipated?

To this question an answer suggested itself which I was tempted to reject, but which haunted me, and would not be dismissed.

The Princess Y— — had arrived in Berlin twelve hours before me. She had come, fully believing that Petrovitch was dead, and prepared to take his place.

She had interviewed Finkelstein, as I knew. Was it not possible that she, also, had been received in the crypt at Potsdam, had been shown the chart of the North Sea, with its ominous red lines, and had accepted the task of launching one of the submarines on its fatal errand?

In spite of all the stories which had been told me of Sophia's daring and resource, in spite of my own experiences of her adventures and reckless proceedings, I did not go so far as to credit her with having proceeded to sea in the missing craft.

But it struck me as altogether in keeping with her character that she should have arranged for the withdrawal of the boat, provided it with a crew, and despatched it fully instructed as to the work to be done.

But whether these suspicions were well founded or

otherwise, of one thing there could be no doubt. A submarine had been taken by some one, and was now on its way to the North Sea, to lie in wait for the ships of Admiral Rojestvensky.

This discovery entirely changed the position for me.

I had come down to Kiel intending to take a submarine out to sea, to watch for the approach of the Russian fleet, and to take whatever steps proved practicable to avert any collision between it and the fishing-boats on the Dogger Bank.

I now saw that the chance of my preventing a catastrophe depended entirely on the movements of the boat which had left already. This boat had become my objective, to use a strategical phrase.

Somewhere in the North Sea was a submarine boat, charged with the mission of provoking a world-wide war. And that boat I had to find.

There was no time to be lost. I hastened back by the most direct way I could find, to the dockyard gates. The little postern was still unlocked, and I passed out, the sentry again taking no notice of my passage.

But at the first street corner I saw a man in seafaring dress who fixed a very keen gaze on me as I came up, and saluted me by touching his cap.

"Good-night," I said in a friendly voice, slowing down in my walk.

"Good-night, sir. Beg pardon, Captain,"—he came and moved along beside me—"but you don't happen to know of a job for a seafaring man, I suppose?"

I stopped dead, and looked him straight in the eyes.

"How many men do you estimate are required to navigate a submarine?" I asked.

"Fifteen," was the prompt answer.

"How soon can you have them here?" was my next question.

The fellow glanced at his watch.

"It's half-past eleven now, Captain. I could collect them and bring them here by half-past one."

"Do it, then," I returned and walked swiftly away.

The whole thing, it was evident, had been prearranged, and I did not choose to waste time in mock negotiations.

I went back to my inn to wait, but there was nothing for me to do, except examine the cartridges in my revolver. I was not quite sure how much my crew had been told, and I thought it just possible that I might have some trouble with them when they found out the nature of my proceedings.

Punctually at the hour fixed I returned to the street outside the dockyard, where I found fifteen men assembled.

Glancing over them, I formed the opinion that they were picked men, on whom I could have relied thoroughly for the work I had been ordered to do, but who might be all the more likely to mutiny if they suspected that I was playing false.

I stood in front of them in the silence of the street.

"Now, my men, if there is any one of you who is not prepared to obey me, even if I order him to scuttle the ship, let him fall out before we start."

Not a man stirred. Not an eyelash quivered. The German discipline had done its work.

"I give you notice that the first man who hesitates to carry out my orders will be shot."

The threat was received with perfect resignation.

"Follow me."

I turned on my heel, and led the way to the dockyard gates, the men marching after me with a regular tramp which could only have been acquired on the deck of a man-of-war.

The sentry was, if possible, more indifferent to our approach than he had been when I had been alone. I threw open the wicket, and bade the last man close it.

Then we marched in the same order to the place where the five submarines were moored.

"I am going on board one of these boats," I announced. "Find something to take us off."

The man whom I had engaged originally, taking on himself the part of mate, repeated my directions. A large whale-boat was found tied up in a convenient spot beside the wharf.

We all got in, and I took the tiller. The mate, who answered to the Russian name of Orloff, though the only language I heard him speak was German, said nothing till I brought the whale-boat alongside of the nearest submarine.

"I beg pardon, Captain, but I have a fancy that the boat at the far end is in better trim, if you have no choice."

"Why didn't you tell me so at once?" I returned sharply, not too well pleased to find him so well informed.

We boarded the submarine pointed out, and found it, of course, provided with everything necessary for an immediate departure, including provisions for a week.

"You understand the navigation of the Canal, I suppose?" I inquired of Orloff.

"I do, sir."

"Very good. Take the boat through. And ascertain all that you can about another submarine which must have passed through yesterday. Wake me if you hear or see anything."

I lay down in the captain's berth and tried to sleep. But the excitement and, I may say, the romantic interest of the adventure proved too strong for me.

I rose again, and came to where my deputy was seated, carefully conning the boat out of the dockyard basin into the Baltic end of the great Canal.

We were already submerged, only the tip of our conning staff being out of the water. But by an ingenious system of tiny mirrors the steersman was able to see his way as plainly as if he had been on deck above the surface.

On approaching the lock by which the basin opened into the Canal, no signal appeared to be given. Silently, as if of their own accord, the huge sluices opened and shut, and we glided out into the great waterway which has made the German Navy independent of Danish good-will.

The voyage along the Kiel Canal in the silence of the night was deeply interesting, and were I not obliged to restrict myself severely to the naked outline of such facts as bear directly on the catastrophe, I should like to attempt a description of the weird and picturesque scene.

Keeping steadily just under the surface, we proceeded swiftly past ports and villages and lonely wharves, till the stars paled and disappeared and a faint flush overspreading the sky in front warned us that day was breaking behind us.

I searched the banks for anything resembling the craft of which I was in search, but in vain. We passed many other ships, chiefly merchantmen bound for Lubeck and Dantzig and other Baltic ports, but of course without being perceived ourselves.

When we reached the mouth of the Canal, I ordered Orloff to stop.

"I must go ashore here, and inquire about the other boat," I explained.

I saw from the expression of his face that this step was not quite to his liking, but he did not venture on any remonstrance.

He brought the boat alongside the bank, and raised her gently to the surface, to enable me to step on shore.

But my quest proved useless, as perhaps I ought to have foreseen.

The harbor-master, or port captain, to whom I addressed myself, affected the most entire ignorance of the exit of any submarine within the last week or more.

"What you suggest is impossible," he assured me. "Every submarine is well known and carefully guarded, and if one had been permitted to leave Kiel by way of the Canal, I should have been notified in advance. No such notification has reached me, and therefore, as you will see, no such boat can possibly have left."

I suspected that he was lying, but I thought it unsafe to persist.

It occurred to me too late that I had been guilty of some imprudence in showing so much anxiety on the subject. It was only too probable that my inquiries would be reported to the Kaiser, who would draw his own inferences in the event of anything going wrong.

I returned on board my own boat, saying nothing to Orloff, and gave the order to proceed.

Orloff had handed over the wheel to one of his subordinates, who steered the submarine out into the blue waters of the North Sea.

As soon as we were well out of reach of the Slesvig shore, I said to the steersman,

"Now I will take the helm."

Instead of promptly relinquishing it to me, the man turned his head in search of Orloff, saying at the same time,

"Do you understand the course, sir?"

I saw that if I meant to be master of the vessel, I must prove that my words of the night before were spoken in earnest. I drew my revolver, and put a bullet through the mutineer's head.

Chapter 32 The Dogger Bank

The sound of the explosion reverberated through the little craft like thunder. Orloff and half a dozen more men came rushing up.

"This man disobeyed me," I said, quietly, slipping a fresh cartridge into the smoking chamber of my revolver. "Throw the body overboard, and return to your duties."

What instructions Orloff and his men had received it was impossible for me to guess. But they clearly did not authorize any breach of discipline at this stage of the voyage.

Without the slightest demur they lifted up the body, and carried it off. I had learned the way to manage the submarine by watching Orloff during the night, and I now pressed a lever which brought us swiftly to the surface. There was a sound of trampling feet overhead, followed by a splash, and I saw the mutineer's body drift past.

It would be idle to seek for words in which to describe the overpowering anxiety which racked my nerves as we tore through the water. The peace of Europe, the safety of Japan and Great Britain, perhaps the future of the world, might be at stake.

Everything depended on my finding the other submarine before it had launched its bolt against the great war fleet which was even now steaming through the Danish Belts, officered by men, some of whom I knew to be ready to take advantage of any pretext for outraging the peace of the seas.

It did not take me long to decide that the neighborhood of the Dogger Bank was the most likely place, in fact the only place, for my search.

I am not wholly unskilled in navigation, having given up a

good deal of my spare time to yachting. With the aid of a chart which was on board, I had little difficulty in keeping a fairly straight course for the famous fishing ground.

On the way I did not neglect the opportunity of acquiring a complete command over the movements of the submarine.

It was driven by electricity, and so designed that by means of various knobs, one man could control it entirely, steering it, raising or lowering it in the water, increasing or slackening speed, stopping, backing, and even discharging the torpedo which was its only weapon of attack—with the exception of a small sharp ram at the bow.

Having asserted my authority, and acquired the practical knowledge I needed, I at last called Orloff to me, and gave him the wheel.

"Take me to the Dogger Bank. Warn me as soon as we get near any fishing-boats, and above all keep a careful lookout for our consort."

It was by this name that I thought it most prudent to refer to the object of my search.

Orloff took the wheel, and said immediately with an air of great respect,

"You have laid a marvelously straight course, Captain. I was not aware that you were familiar with these waters. The Dogger Bank is right ahead, and we shall reach it in less than an hour."

An hour later I was conscious of a light shock as the submarine stopped.

We had grounded on the sandy shoal of the Dogger, in twenty fathoms of water, and overhead I could see great black shadows sweeping slowly past.

They were cast by the trawlers of the Gamecock fleet.

It being still daylight I did not venture to let the submarine show itself on the surface of the sea.

Hugging the bottom, I steered in and out among the great trailing nets of the fisher fleet.

At the same time I ordered my crew to keep a sharp watch for the first submarine, promising fifty marks[1] to the man who sighted her.

The rest of that day passed without anything happening.

As soon as darkness fell I brought my boat up to the surface, partly in order to renew the air supply, and partly to scan the horizon in search of the oncoming Russian fleet.

But thanks to the promptness with which I had gone out to sea I had anticipated Rojestvensky by twenty-four hours. The Baltic Fleet was still in Danish waters, waiting to pick up the German pilots who were to lure it from its course.

Finding there were no signs of the Russians, I submerged the submarine, all except the little conning tube, which was invisible in the darkness, and ran in among the English smacks.

As I heard the brave, hardy fishermen talking to one another, the temptation was a strong one to disclose myself, and warn them of the coming peril.

Only my experience of the uselessness of such warnings restrained me. I knew that these simple, law-abiding citizens would laugh me in the face if I told them that they were in danger from the warships of a foreign Power.

As my unseen vessel glided softly past the side of one fishing-boat, whose name I could just make as the *Crane*, I overheard a few scraps of conversation, which threw a pathetic light on the situation.

"We shall have the Rooshians coming along presently," said one voice.

"No," answered another, "they won't come anywhere near us. 'Tis out of their course."

"They do say the Rooshians don't know much about seamanship," a third voice spoke out. "Like as not we'll see their search-lights going by."

"Well, if they come near enough, we'll give the beggars a cheer; what d'ye say?"

"Aye, let's. Fair play's what I wishes 'em, and let the best man win."

The words died away along the water, as I drew off and let my craft sink under once again.

That night I slept soundly, making up for the vigil of the night before. The submarine rested on the sea floor, in a hollow of the undulating Bank, and one of the crew kept watch in case a "trawl" should come too close.

But there was no sign of the mysterious companion which had come out of Kiel Harbor in front of me, and was even now prowling somewhere in the dark depths around.

Chapter 33 Trafalgar Day

In the morning I was conscious of a certain stir and display on board some of the fishing boats among which I continued to lurk.

At first I supposed that the Baltic Fleet must have been sighted. But in the course of the day I gathered from various cries and shouts which were borne across the water, that the fishermen were keeping the anniversary of the most glorious day in the history of England, the day on which the immortal Nelson annihilated the united fleets of France and Spain, and shattered the dream of the great Napoleon that he could tame the haughty Island Power.

As long as daylight lasted I scoured the sea for a distance of five miles all around the devoted fishing fleet, without coming on the slightest trace of the other submarine.

A delusive hope assailed me that some accident might have overtaken it. But I did not relax my vigilance, and when night fell I took up a station about a mile in front of the English smacks, in the direction from which I had reason to expect the approach of Rojestvensky.

A few hours elapsed, then my watchfulness was rewarded.

Away down on the horizon toward the northeast, there glittered out a row of twinkling lights, one behind the other, as though a lamp-lit thoroughfare had got afloat and drifted out to sea.

The sinuous streak of lights, shifting as they approached like the coils of some great water-snake, glided toward us at what seemed a fearful speed, and as they drew near the white lights were interspread with green and crimson points, like rubies and emeralds set between rows of diamonds. And ever and anon the swift electric tongues of the search-lights spat forth and licked the dark face of the waters like hungry things.

Keeping my upper deck just awash, I lay still and beheld at last the great black sides of the battleships tower up, pierced with illuminated windows.

My heart began to throb wildly. If only the other submarine failed to appear; if only the English fishermen would realize their danger and flee in time, disaster might be averted.

The hope had scarcely formed itself in my mind when Orloff, who had come to repose confidence in me, respectfully touched my arm and pointed ahead.

Not two hundred yards from me, stealing along about a mile in advance of the Russian fleet, I perceived a small dark object, showing hardly a foot above the surface of the waves.

It was the rival submarine!

Instead of proceeding direct to the Dogger Bank, as I had done, the other boat must have joined Admiral Rojestvensky's squadron, and come on before it like a jackal pointing out the lion's prey.

"Go forward," I commanded the German mate. "Let no one disturb me till this business is over."

Orloff gave me a wondering look, but obeyed without an instant's hesitation.

As soon as his back was turned, I swung the wheel around, put on the full power of the engines, and went after the craft I had been searching for during the last forty-eight hours.

Had the commander of the other submarine noticed mine, and did he suspect my intention to frustrate his design? It almost seemed so. His boat, scarcely visible in the gloom, fled in front of me to where the foremost fishing boats were riding lazily over the shoals, dragging their nets along the bottom.

It was a weird chase. Neither of us showed a glint of light, or made the smallest sound. Like two great shadowing fish we darted through the depths of the sea, hunter and hunted.

In between the sagging nets with their load of cod and flounders, shot the phantom boat I was pursuing, and I followed, obliged to slacken speed as we twisted in and out under the keels of the unconscious fishermen.

And all this time the huge warships in two lines astern were plunging through the seas, heading straight for the unfortunate smacks.

The chase seemed to be aware that it was a case of now or never. I was catching up with it fast; I was able to mark its course by the broken water churned up by its propeller; when, all at once, I saw it rise with the swift motion of a bird.

I had no alternative but to do the same.

As I emerged upon the surface I found my boat in the very center of the full glare of a search-light which lit up the whole scene with dazzling radiance.

Fresh from the depths below, where all had been dark, my eyes fairly blinked in the sudden splendor of light.

Then, for what might have been from three to five seconds, I saw everything that passed.

The foremost vessels of the Russian fleet had already gone past the group of drifting trawlers. One large cruiser was passing within a stone's-throw of the nearest fishing-boat, and the English fishermen were playfully holding up some of their freshly-caught fish, as though offering it to the Russian sailors.

Another line of warships was coming up behind, with its search-lights thrown out in front.

And then, right across the range of lights, and in a straight line between the Russian battleships and the English smacks, I saw the phantom torpedo boat pass deliberately, as high out of the water as she could show.

What happened next took place so swiftly, and with such confusion that I cannot pretend to describe it with accuracy.

Shouts rang out on some of the Russian ships, the submarine headed around as though to seek refuge among the trawlers, and then a gun was fired, and a cannon-ball struck the water within a few feet of me.

All at once, it seemed to me, and as though by some preconcerted plan, half the ships of the Baltic Fleet opened fire on the English fishermen, who seemed too surprised and horrified to do anything. I saw ball after ball crash into one luckless smack, which quickly began to fill and sink. But, generally speaking, the marksmanship of the Russians was too wild for the firing to have serious effect.

As soon as I realized that I had become a mark for the Russian guns I sank beneath the surface. It is no doubt this voluntary move on my part which has given rise to the belief cherished by some of the officers of the Baltic Fleet, and indorsed by Admiral Rojestvensky, that a torpedo boat was sunk by their fire.

But I knew that the massacre—for it was nothing less—would go on as long as the other submarine remained on the surface, mixing among the luckless fishing boats with the deliberate intention of drawing on them the Russian fire.

I marked her course, put my engines to their fullest speed

one more, and rushed after her.

This time my coming was not watched by the hostile commander. Like Admiral Rojestvensky, he may have believed that my boat had been sunk by the ball which had come so close. Or else, perhaps, in his exultation at having brought about an event which seemed to make war inevitable, he had forgotten his former fears.

But the truth will never be known.

I brought my own boat right under the demon craft, and then, tilting her up at a sharp angle, rammed the other in the center of her keel.

There was a concussion, a muffled sound of tearing iron, and as I backed away at full speed astern, I saw the waters of the North Sea pour through a long jagged rent in the bottom of the doomed submarine, and watched her go down staggering like a wounded vulture through the air.

The shock of the collision had brought Orloff and the rest of my crew running aft.

"An accident," I explained coolly. "I have sunk some boat or other in the dark."

The men exchanged suspicious glances.

"It was the other submarine, sir," said Orloff, still preserving his respectful tone. "Will you permit us to see whether it is possible to save any of the crew?"

"Do as you please," I returned, leaving the helm. "My work here is done, and I am ready to go back."

I intended them to think I referred to the attack on the fishing-boats. The cannonade died away as I spoke.

We went down through the water to where the wrecked submarine was lying half over on her side. Some frightened faces peered at us out of the upper portholes, where a supply of air still lingered.

It was impossible to do anything for them down there without being swamped ourselves. We could only invite them by signs to forsake their own craft and let us carry them up to the surface where it would be safe for us to take them inside.

In order to receive them on our upper deck we circled slowly around to the opposite side of their vessel. And there I beheld a sight which will haunt me for years to come.

The whole side of the submarine had been wrenched open, revealing the interior of the cabin. And on the floor, lying in the peaceful attitude of one who had just resigned herself to sleep, I beheld the drowned form of the beautiful, desperate, perhaps wicked, but unhappy, woman from whose mad love I had fled.

So, in the midst of the wild North Sea, in their strange coffin, the bones of Sophia, Princess Yernoloff, lie and rock on the incessant tides that sweep across the Dogger Bank.

Requiescat in pace!

As our boat, laden with the rescued survivors, shot up again to the surface, I felt a noosed rope drawn tightly around my throat and heard the voice of Orloff hiss in my ear,

"I arrest you in the name of the Kaiser!"

Chapter 34 *The Family Statute*

My task is done. At last the reader knows all that ever will be known—all there is to know, in short—concerning the tragedy of the North Sea.

My personal adventures can possess little interest after the all-important transactions I have had to describe. But in case there should be a reader here and there who is good enough to feel any curiosity as to my fate, I will briefly tell what followed on my arrest.

My revolver was taken from me and I was conducted under a strict guard back to Kiel.

Off the mouth of the Canal we were boarded by a despatch-boat flying the German naval ensign, and a police officer with three men took me off the submarine.

The first proceeding of my new captor was to handcuff me. He then warned me,

"If you speak a single word to me or any one else till you are in the imperial presence, my orders are to shoot you through the head."

I nodded. I had as little wish to speak as the Emperor could have to let me. My thoughts were busy with the memory of the woman of whose tragic death I had been the unwitting cause, and with the measures that remained to be taken to extenuate, so far as extenuation was possible, the fatal action of the Baltic fleet.

As for myself, I can say truly that I had become almost indifferent to what was in store for me. My feeling toward the unfortunate Princess had not been such as that which makes a man desire a woman for his wife; it had not deserved the name of love, perhaps; and it was certainly free from any taint of a less noble passion.

Nevertheless it had been a powerful sentiment, colored and strengthened by my knowledge of her love for me.

Sophia had loved me. She had saved my life. And I had taken hers in return.

Must I accuse myself of weakness for feeling as if happiness for me were over, and the best fate I could wish would be to lie there beside my victim on the lonely Dogger sands?

When I came before Wilhelm II. he was not in the Hall of the Hohenzollerns, indulging his vein of extravagant romance, but in his private cabinet and in his most stern and business-like mood.

"Give the prisoner a chair, and wait outside," his majesty commanded briefly.

I sat down, still handcuffed, and the guards withdrew.

"Now," said the Kaiser, fixing me with an eagle glance, "be good enough to explain your proceedings."

I met his look with a steadfast one in return.

"I have carried out your majesty's orders scrupulously. I have taken out the submarine torpedo boat, engaged a crew, proceeded to the Dogger Bank, and drawn the fire of the Baltic Fleet on the fishing-boats from Hull. I have not seen a newspaper since, but I assume that the British Navy has already arrested Admiral Rojestvensky and his squadron, and that the two Powers are at war."

The Kaiser gnawed his moustache.

"Things have not gone quite so well as you pretend, M. Petrovitch.

"The Russian cannonade ceased after a few minutes," the

Emperor resumed. "You did not remain on the surface after the first shot; you did not launch your torpedo, neither did you permit the other submarine to do so. In fact you sunk her."

"I had no orders with respect to another submarine, sire. I was entitled to treat it as an enemy."

"Nonsense, you know that it had left Kiel before you, on the same errand."

"On the contrary, sire, I could not possibly know anything of the kind."

"Why, you saw it had disappeared from the dock. You inquired after it along the Canal. When you got out to the Dogger you were searching for it the whole time."

"And when I found it, sire, it was leading the Russian squadron, of which it appeared to form part. I had every right to assume that it was a Russian man-of-war."

"A German boat!" thundered the Kaiser.

"A boat not flying any flag must be presumed to belong to the country of those who are in control of it. I found this submarine under the control of a Russian subject."

"The Princess was my agent."

"Your majesty had not told me so. On the contrary, I understood that you wished my own boat to be considered a Russian vessel, in case of any question. I shipped a Russian crew therefore."

Wilhelm II. frowned angrily.

"Do not play with me, M. Petrovitch. I know all about your crew. Explain why you, a Russian subject, should have attacked what you are pleased to pretend was a Russian ship."

"I regret to have to say that your majesty is laboring under a mistake. I am not a Russian subject."

This time the Kaiser was fairly taken aback.

"What subject are you?"

"A Japanese."

Wilhelm looked thunderstruck.

"Japanese!" was all he could say.

"If your majesty pleases. That being so, as soon as I took possession of the submarine, with your permission, of course it became a Japanese ship."

"What you tell me is monstrous—ridiculous. Your name is Russian, your face is at least European."

"My name, sire, is Matsukata. I received it in Tokio at the commencement of the war, on being adopted into a Japanese family.

"If your majesty doubts my statement, I ask to be confronted with the Japanese Ambassador in Berlin."

The Kaiser looked as if he would have liked to doubt it, but found himself unable to do so.

"Then on your own showing you are a Japanese spy," he pronounced slowly. "As such I am entitled to have you shot."

"Pardon me again, sire. In Petersburg I admit, that was my character. In Germany I have been your majesty's agent, and have literally fulfilled your commands."

"You are a very acute quibbler, I see," was the retort, "but quibbles will not save you. You have stolen one of my ships to sink another with, and at the very least you deserve to be hanged as a pirate."

"I demand to be tried," I said boldly, knowing that this was the one step to which the Emperor, for his own sake, could not consent.

As I expected, he frowned uneasily.

"In this case I must exercise my right of refusing a civil trial, in the interest of the State. I will give you a court-martial with closed doors."

"That would be illegal, sire."

"You dare to tell me so!"

"Your majesty will find I am right. The case falls within the Hohenzollern Family Statute."

The Kaiser appeared stupefied.

"The Family Statute?" he repeated slowly, as if unable to believe his ears. "What has the Statute to do with you?"

"It is provided in the Statute, if I recollect rightly, sire, that a member of the Imperial Family can be tried only by his peers, that is to say, by a court composed of members of your majesty's House."

"Well, and what then?"

"By another clause in the Statute—I regret that the number has escaped my memory—the privileges of a Hohenzollern in that respect are extended to members of other reigning Houses."

"What are you going to tell me?" Wilhelm II. demanded in amazement.

"Only that I have the honor to be the adopted son of his imperial highness Prince Yorimo, cousin to his majesty the Emperor of Japan."

The German monarch sat still, unable to parry this unexpected blow.

"The Japanese Ambassador—" he began to mutter.

"Will confirm my statement, sire. I have already asked to be confronted with him. Before going to Kiel, I sent him information of my plans, so that he is already expecting to hear from me, I have no doubt."

Wilhelm II. saw that he had come to the end of his tether. Lying back in his chair, he ejaculated— —

"I believed there was only one man in the two hemispheres who could do things like this!"

"I am flattered to think you may be right, sire," I responded in my natural voice, with a smile.

The Emperor bounded from his seat.

"You—are—Monsieur V— —!" he fairly gasped out.

"I was, sire. Permit me to repeat that I am now called Prince Matsukata of Japan."

Wilhelm II. made an effort, and came out of it with his best manner.

"Then, in that case, you will stay and lunch with the Empress and myself, my dear Prince."

As soon as the handcuffs had been removed, I told the whole story to the Kaiser, who was immensely interested, and decidedly touched by the part which related to the drowned Princess.

Before leaving the Palace, I asked permission of my imperial host to make use of his private wire for a message to London, in the interest of peace.

Wilhelm II., who began to see that he had been betrayed into going a little farther than was altogether desirable, consented in the friendliest spirit, merely stipulating that he should be allowed to see the message.

He was rather surprised when he found it was addressed to Lord Bedale at Buckingham Palace, and comprised a single word, "Elsinore."

And so, although some of the newspapers in the two

capitals of England and Russia continued to breathe war for some days longer, I felt no more anxiety after reading the paragraph which stated that the British Prime Minister, at the close of the decisive Cabinet Council, had driven to the Palace to be received in private audience by her majesty Queen Alexandra.

Epilogue

As I write these lines the war which has cost so many brave lives, and carried so much desolation through the fields and cities of Manchuria is still raging.

The great fleet of Admiral Rojestvensky, from which the stains of the innocent fisherman's blood have not yet been washed, is plowing its way to meet a terrible retribution at the hands of the victorious Togo.[2] A curse is on that fleet, and it may be that the British Government foresaw that they could punish the crime of the Dogger Bank more terribly by letting it proceed, than by bringing it into Portsmouth to await the result of the international trial.

In the great affairs of nations it is not always wise to exact strict justice, or to expose the actual truth.

I, too, am a lover of peace. Not of that hysterical, sentimental horror of bloodshed which would place a great civilized nation at the mercy of more barbarous powers, which would stay the wheels of progress, and be indistinguishable from cowardice in the face of wrong.

But I am a friend of the peace which is the natural result of a better understanding between peoples, of respect for one another's character and aims, of a wise recognition of facts, and an honorable determination not to play the part of the aggressor.

It is in the hope of promoting such a peace on earth, and such good-will toward men, that I have allowed myself to publish the foregoing narrative.

In order to soften the character of this revelation I have endeavored to impart to it a character of romance.

So far as my abilities extend, I have sought to give the reader the impression that he has been reading an allegory rather than a dry, business record. I have tried to cover certain incidents with a discreet veil. I have as much as possible refrained from using real names.

I trust that my narration will be accepted in the spirit in which it has been written and that no reader will allow his feelings of curiosity to lead him into going further, or raising questions which it might be indiscreet on my part to answer.

But there is one part of the story to which the foregoing remarks do not apply.

Whatever else be mythical, there is nothing mythical about the bright figure whose portrait has accompanied me through so many perils. There is a home for me in far-off Tokio, and when the blood-begrimed battalions of Asia sheathe their swords, I shall go thither to claim my reward.

[1] A silver mark is about twenty cents of our money. [2] These words, which have been proven prophetic, were written last March, when Admiral Rojestvensky's fleet was still a very formidable fact to be reckoned with. — Editor.

Lightning Source UK Ltd.
Milton Keynes UK
UKHW020109220219
337759UK00010B/1047/P